Savage Bandits

Longarm was sprayed by exploding sand. All around him hot lead was pounding into the ground, each salvo getting uncomfortably closer. A cry came from Longarm's right and Wynne toppled over. Surprisingly, Pettigrew seemed unafraid. He loaded his Springfield with calm deliberateness and with the same care returned fire, round after methodical round.

And then the Mexicans were among them, charging recklessly through the camp, overturning their tents, kicking aside their cooking utensils. Out of ammunition, Longarm used his rifle as a club and, with a wild swing of the long barrel, knocked the closest *bandito* out of his saddle. Another flung himself off his horse and slammed Longarm to the ground under him, his bowie held high. Longarm rolled over, caught the man's wrist, and twisted. The wrist snapped like a dry twig...

TABOR EVANS

LONGARM

AND THE DESERT SPIRITS

A JOVE BOOK

LONGARM AND THE DESERT SPIRITS

A Jove Book/published by arrangement with
the author

PRINTING HISTORY
Jove edition/March 1987

ISBN: 0-515-08907-9

Jove Books are published by the Berkley Publishing Group,
200 Madison Avenue, New York, NY 10016.
The words "A JOVE BOOK" and the "J" with sunburst
are trademarks belonging to Jove Publications, Inc.

PRINTED IN THE UNITED STATES OF AMERICA

Chapter 1

Longarm awoke to the feel of a woman's curl tickling his upturned nostril. He opened his eyes and brushed aside the long strand of hair. It smelled vaguely of smoke and whiskey and belonged to a lady of the night who had brought him luck at the gaming tables the night before. He sat up and looked at her. Her name was Vivian. She didn't look nearly as good as she had the night before when she had been wreathed in pipe and cigar smoke and was continually bending over his table, her magnificent cleavage on display for all to admire.

Now the cold morning light was treating her rouged countenance and the lines in her neck with unnecessary cruelty. As Longarm flung aside his covers and stood naked on bare feet beside the bed, he looked back down at her.

1

"You awake, Vivian?"

She opened only one eye. "'What time's it?"

Padding over to the top of his dresser, Longarm consulted his watch. "Time to rise and shine. Seven o'clock."

"Oh, my God," she said.

She pulled the covers over her head and turned to the wall, mumbling something about waking her at noon. Grinning, Longarm said nothing more to her and dressed himself as quickly as possible.

A bottle of Maryland rye sat on the dresser top in front of him. It had only a heel left. He tipped up the bottle, squished it around to clean off his teeth some, then swallowed the belt. It hit his empty stomach with the force of a locomotive pitching off a trestle. He wiped his mouth and started dressing.

Soon after, with his Colt in his cross-draw holster and his sneaky derringer in his watch-fob pocket, Longarm settled his flat-crowned Stetson onto his crisp hair and, with a twirl of his mustache, marched out to confront the world. As he closed his door behind him, he did not look back at his night's companion. He had no doubt she had awakened in other rooms on other mornings and would have no difficulty. He figured she would wake up at noon or later, sit blearily for a while on the edge of the bed and stare out at a day already half gone and scratch her hair, then dress and leave, with no pleasant conversation or warm goodbye to speed her on her way.

It was not a pleasant image, and shards of it clung to Longarm as he sought out the greasy spoon where he usually ate. After his second cup of coffee, he lit his first cheroot of the day—he was trying to cut down—

2

and headed for George Masters's barbershop.

Settled back in the big chair, his long torso covered with a neatly pressed pin-stripe sheet, his head comfortably back on the head rest, he relaxed as George carefully laid the hot, steamed cloth on his face, then brushed onto his chin and neck a rich, scented lather. With swift, deft strokes, George's razor scraped off the hard blue scrub, his pink fingers gently pulling back the skin so as not to impede the long blade's passage over the only face and neck God would ever allot to Custis Long.

Half an hour later, shaved and trimmed, his tanned jaws still cool from the bay rum George applied just before whipping off the striped sheet, Longarm was ready to see what Billy Vail had in store for him this morning. Something that would get him out of Denver soon, he hoped. The mile-high city was beginning to wear on him and that rouged woman back there sleeping in his bed was just one more reminder that he needed a change of scenery.

Two hard-eyed customers stepped out of an alley in front of him, their legs spread, their sixguns out—both yawning muzzles aimed at Longarm's gut. He recognized them: Ma Titus and her son, Clem. Ma was smaller than Clem by a couple of feet. Her hair was gray, her face a pale, wrinkled prune. On the tip of her nose hung a pair of spectacles. As she stood in front of Longarm, holding the big Colt on him, she was forced to lean her head back some so she could see Longarm. The huge brim of her black Stetson was in her way.

Ma Titus motioned Longarm into the alley. Longarm followed her bidding and stepped into the narrow, sunless place. Ma followed in after him, and beside Ma,

3

Clem followed, moistening his lips nervously. They were thin and trembling. His face was gaunt, his eyes furtive and lost in dark hollows. His hair, sticking out from under his black, floppy-brimmed hat, resembled sticks of moldy hay. Both of them stank of horseflesh and horse manure and the sweat that comes of hard riding. They probably hadn't had a bath in a couple of months, at least.

"Got you now, you son of a bitch!" snapped Ma, sending a dagger of tobacco juice out of one corner of her mouth.

"Yes, we have!" echoed Clem, grinning like an idiot.

"Shut up, son."

"Now, hold on here," said Longarm. "You got no call to come after me, Ma. What harm have I ever done you?"

"You kilt my boy, Alf!"

"He came at me with a rifle, knocked me down the side of a canyon. He was trying to beat my brains out with a boulder when I brought him down."

"Yeah," said Ma, "with a derringer. Weren't fair! He didn't know you carried that sissy gun!"

"You think I should carry a sign to advertise the fact?"

"It don't make no matter now."

Ma lifted her revolver and aimed, the tip of her tongue sliding along her upper lip, her ancient eyes squinting.

"Now, hold it, Ma!" Longarm warned.

"Stand back, Clem! I'm a-goin' to do it!"

"Maybe we better wait, Ma!"

"Wait, shit!"

Longarm moved like lightning. He ducked low,

hurled himself at Clem, and knocked him into Ma. Twisting Clem's weapon out of his grasp, Longarm clubbed him on the side of the head with it. Clem went down, grunting softly when his ass slammed onto the wet, cobblestoned surface of the alley. Ma was gone, racing out of the alley, her gun holstered, her right hand holding onto her huge hat.

Longarm tore out of the alley after her. Ma was weaving between the swarm of people on their way to work. Longarm paid them no heed and they peeled quickly to one side as he charged through them. Ma ducked out onto the street. A beer wagon drawn by four immense Belgian horses nearly plowed her under, but she ducked deftly aside and a moment later—with Longarm hot on her heels—she gained the sidewalk on the other side of the street.

Longarm hurdled a newsboy and kept after Ma. A tall, thin woman turned to confront him, her face beet-red with indignation that he should be chasing this poor little old lady. The woman had an umbrella in her hand. As Longarm swept past her, she struck him with it—not once, but twice.

Ma stumbled, then sprawled face down along the sidewalk. Longarm swooped down and plucked Ma off the ground. Ma swung on him, her tiny fist catching him in the stomach. He hardly felt a thing.

Then a hard, vicious blow struck at him from behind. Still hanging on to Ma, Longarm turned. He had ex-pected to see the woman with the umbrella. Instead he was being confronted by two well-dressed gentlemen, one his age, the other considerably older, in his early fifties. The younger gentleman, the man who had struck him in the back of the neck, now stepped forward and

5

caught Longarm on the point of his chin. The blow landed with such force that Longarm let go of Ma and staggered back.

Rushing past Longarm, the two gentlemen rushed to Ma's side, uttering their condolences for Longarm's unseemly behavior. They brushed her off, handed her a dollar bill, and sent her on her way. Ma wasted no time. She vanished at once beyond the ranks of curious onlookers who now crowded close about Longarm.

Still somewhat groggy, and very angry, Longarm tapped the younger man on his shoulder. The fellow turned. Longarm's punch caught him just above his belt. The young man doubled over, gasping in pain. Then Longarm brought up his knee, catching the gent under the right eye. With a muffled cry, he flipped backward but did not go down. That suited Longarm. He strode quickly forward and caught the man on the point of his chin, following through so completely that his right shoulder brushed the back of the man's head as the poor fellow spun about completely and collapsed face down onto the sidewalk.

Then Longarm turned on his older companion.

Red-faced with rage at what Longarm had just done to his companion, the older man flung up his fists in a proper Marquis of Queensberry stance.

Longarm took pity on the older man and did not take the challenge. "Who the hell are you two, anyway?" he asked.

"I should ask that question of you!" the man blustered.

Longarm reached into the inner pocket of his brown frock coat and took out his wallet. As he flashed his badge, he said, "I'll ask you once more. Who the hell are you two?"

"We are . . . visitors to Denver."

"You been here long?"

"We arrived from Boston last night."

"That little old lady you helped escape has probably murdered at least five people—and she just got finished trying to add me to her list. I would have been able to apprehend her if you two hadn't happened along."

"We didn't know," the man said unhappily.

"I suggest you get back on that train and take it all the way back to Boston. You are not welcome in Denver."

"Why, sir, I resent that—exceedingly."

His younger companion got slowly to his feet, shaking his head groggily as he did so. He had seen Longarm's badge and had heard his explanation. The young man looked thoroughly crestfallen.

"Never mind, Dad," he said. "I think we'd better get back to the hotel so I can clean up. That meeting's at nine, don't forget."

The two men hurried off.

As Longarm watched them go, he chuckled. He had not taken their names or hauled them in to charge them with obstructing justice because he knew they had only been trying to help what they saw as a little old lady being worked over by an uncouth ruffian. Their instincts were good. In the future, it would behoove them both to keep out of any disturbance that did not concern them, at least until they got some idea of where they were. This wasn't Boston. This was the Wild West.

As Longarm had expected, when he got back to the alley, he found that Clem had picked himself up and was gone, like his mother. Longarm shrugged. There was no need to worry. They would be back to nail him some other time. And, meanwhile, Longarm had an appointment with Billy Vail.

He glanced at his pocketwatch and swore, his long strides hurrying him on toward Colfax Avenue.

"Where in blazes have you been?" Billy Vail demanded.

"You wouldn't believe it, so I won't tell you."

"That suits me just fine." Billy shoved a folder at Longarm across his cluttered desk.

Longarm leaned forward in the red morocco chair and took the folder. Flipping through it, he saw letter after letter of introduction. He glanced quickly through each one, but it was the signatures at the bottom of the letters that interested him the most. Every single letter bore the name of a mighty big chief, if titles meant anything. Most of them were either connected with or mighty interested in the Smithsonian Institution. The gist of it was that an expedition was on its way to a dig in the middle of Pima Indian land, and it was hoped that the Denver office would see to it that a competent federal marshal would go along to make sure the expedition reached its destination safely and was able to go about its business of digging up old Indian graves.

Handing the folder back to Billy, Longarm had a premonitory chill. He had wet-nursed Washington bigwigs before. These archaeologists mentioned in the letters were probably smart enough, but sometimes scientists had their heads a mite too high into the clouds—for their own good and for the good of anyone fool enough to be along for the ride.

"Spell it out, Billy," Longarm said. "I got to wipe the

8

noses of some more danged scientists. Ain't that it?"

"Yep. Sorry."

"Then I'll need more details."

"You mean you'll go along with this assignment, Custis?"

Longarm grinned at Billy and leaned back in the chair. "Sure, I will, Billy. I'm getting tired of horse manure sticking to my boots, and smoky back rooms and women that hide behind powder and lipstick. Hell, I'd escort an angel on a tour of hell if it would get me out of here. But first, Billy, like I just told you, I need a few more details."

"Grab your hat and we'll get out of here," Billy replied, relieved. "We'll get all the details you need in a few minutes. The delegation mentioned in that folder arrived last night. I met them at the station. They're staying at the Warren Hotel. We're supposed to meet them there this morning."

Longarm grunted amiably and followed Billy out of the office.

After his sharp rap on the door, Marshal Vail preceded Longarm into the hotel room. Longarm came to a halt in the middle of the room, staring in some disbelief at the two men waiting for them. He was confronting the two men he had had the altercation with less than an hour before on the streets of Denver.

Billy closed the hotel room door and pulled up beside Longarm.

"Gentlemen," he said, "I want you to meet Deputy Marshal Custis Long, known to his friends as Longarm. He'll be escorting you into the Sonora country."

"That so?" said the older man.

9

"Hello, Mr. Long," the young man said, extending his arm. "A pleasure to meet you again. I'm Nathan Pettigrew. This is my father, Edward."

Edward stepped forward and extended his hand. Longarm shook it casually, then looked back at Nathan. The young gentleman's jaw was swollen, and there was a growing bruise on his forehead, which must have been caused when he hit the sidewalk face down.

"How're you feeling?" Longarm asked, grinning slightly.

"Not so good, I must admit."

Marshal Vail looked from Longarm to the other two. It was apparent to him that these three had met before, and that the circumstances had not been altogether amicable. "What's going on here?" he asked Longarm.

"We've already met, Billy," Longarm admitted. "This morning."

"Where?"

"Not far from Colfax."

The young man laughed nervously and broke in. "Your deputy had caught up with a rather wizened old woman and was shaking her up pretty bad, when Dad and I sort of rode to the rescue. When the smoke cleared, Marshal Long was minus the little old lady and I was picking myself up off the sidewalk."

"It was a regrettable error," said Edward Pettigrew. "Nate and I had no idea the marshal was a law officer."

Vail turned to Longarm. "Explain."

When Longarm finished, there were lines of concern etched on Vail's face. "Damn it, Longarm. You better watch it. That Ma Titus is getting meaner with each new gray hair. We been getting word on her and that half-wit son of hers. They've joined the Wilmer Gang, as mean a bunch of coyotes as ever got loose."

"Then the marshal wasn't exaggerating? That old woman *was* really dangerous?" the elder Pettigrew asked.

Vail nodded grimly. "She's gone past dangerous long since. Right now I'd say she's got a heart of pure granite and the instincts of a treed cougar."

Nathan looked at Longarm and shook his head sadly. "We certainly do owe you an apology," he said.

"Forget it," said Longarm. "You had the right instincts, just the wrong granny."

"I suggest we get down to business," said the elder Pettigrew, moving two chairs over to a table. "I've sent for coffee, gentlemen. It should be here shortly."

As the four men sat down, the coffee arrived. It was Nathan who explained things.

Nate's father—the leader of the expedition—was out to prove that the fabled Hohokum People, who once settled the land where the Pima Indians now lived, were descendants of a higher race—perhaps survivors from the Lost Continent of Atlantis. From what Pettigrew knew of the present-day Pima culture and the Pima Indians themselves, it seemed to him highly unlikely that they could possibly be descendants of this brilliant race of pre-historical engineers who had been able to wrest from a barren stretch of desert a more than bountiful existence.

"And how do you intend to prove this theory?" Longarm asked.

"By digging, Marshal," Pettigrew replied, somewhat pompously. "We are archaeologists. We find a likely spot, search for ruins, dig carefully, sift the artifacts, and are thus able to piece together much of what the ancient civilizations were all about."

Longarm smiled. "Like Schliemann at Troy."

11

Pettigrew looked at Longarm in some astonishment. "Oh! You've heard about that, have you?"

"I have a secret vice. I read."

Nathan chuckled.

"What concerns me," Longarm went on, "is that you're expecting the Pima tribes to let you walk in and start digging up their sacred land, what they call the land of their spirits."

Billy Vail chuckled. "That's why you've been roped in," he explained. "We're hoping the Pimas will listen to you explain how it is."

"And just how *is* it?"

"Washington, that is, the BIA, has given its approval, and you know they can do whatever they want with Pima land, even if it is on the Pima reservation."

"And you think the Pimas will go along."

"Depends, Longarm. You've had experience down there, I seem to recall. That's what we're all counting on," Vail told him.

Longarm took a deep breath and looked back at the two archaeologists. "I can't promise you anything for sure," he told them. "But I'll do my best."

"But what's the fuss?" Pettigrew demanded. "As I understand it, not one single white man has ever died at the hands of a Pima warrior."

"There's always a first time."

"But from all I've heard, they are a peaceful, agrarian people!"

Longarm grinned. "Sure, they're peaceful. Like bees happily filling a hive. But I wouldn't advise poking your head into that hive."

Billy Vail cleared his throat. "You've heard of Apaches?"

Both of the Easterners acknowledged they had.

"Apaches steer a wide course around the Pimas—and them's the only tribe I know that Apaches fear."

"I see," said Pettigrew. "Well, then. We will most assuredly be grateful for any help you can render, Marshal."

At that moment the door opened and two men and a woman entered. Longarm got to his feet and found himself trying not to stare at the woman as she paused in the center of the room to take off her wide, sweeping brimmed hat. Dressed in a long, cool, apple-red skirt, and a white blouse with ruffles at the neck and sleeves, she was stunning. Her classic features were clean, yet delicately cast. She had magnificent dark brown eyes, and a rich corona of auburn hair piled on top of her head. As he watched her slim, willowy figure glide toward him, Longarm found himself imagining her loosening that hair and letting it tumble down over her naked breasts.

Unsettled somewhat by the image he was conjuring, Longarm felt fine beads of sweat standing out on his forehead. He did his best to pull himself together as he kept track of the introduction. These three newcomers, together with Nathan and his father, made up the body of the expedition. All of them, it appeared, were archaeologists. The woman was Roberta Prescott, and the young man with her was her brother, James. Longarm shook hands with Roberta and found the clasp firm and her smile warm. He was then introduced to the second young man who had entered the room with her. He was Wynne Pettigrew, Nathan's younger brother, and as he shook Wynne's hand, Longarm was informed that Wynne and Roberta were engaged.

13

Sighing inwardly, Longarm decided he would just have to hold himself in check during this expedition—if he could.

Three days later they were five miles from Lizard Gulch where they had disembarked from the train, and already the Sonora desert had swallowed them up. They made a sizable party, with six heavily laden mules, and four digger Indians to serve as porters, as Edward Pettigrew insisted on calling them. Longarm had had no say in their employment, and he did not like it. The diggers were notorious thieves. If they weren't exceedingly careful, Pettigrew and his party would be lucky to return with all their teeth remaining in their heads.

Roberta spurred her horse forward until she was alongside Longarm. Then she pulled up to keep pace with him. He glanced over at her and smiled.

"How're you doing?"

"Fine. But isn't this terrible country?"

He shrugged. She had refused to ride sidesaddle and was forking her horse like a man, wearing a pair of Levi's and a man's checked shirt, with the sleeves rolled up past her elbows. After the first day, her fair complexion had turned red and her arms had been burned almost raw. She had ignored the pain and gone uncomplainingly to her tent. Now her arms, face, and neck were as dark as an Indian's.

"It's terrible country for us, but the Pimas don't mind. Neither do the sidewinders, the Gila monsters, and the beaded lizards. Then there's the scorpions. They don't mind it, either."

"If you think you can discourage me, you're mistaken."

"I don't think anything could discourage you," he told her.

"It's nice of you to say that," she remarked, pleased.

Then she sat back in her saddle and relaxed while she rode beside him, quietly competent, no longer needing to chatter. He found that he enjoyed her alert, silent company.

They were riding through a brush-covered desert land dotted with huge saguaro cactus. It was gently rolling country for the most part, but Longarm caught sight of occasional lava flats and rimrock, and the ground over which they rode was gravelly, lightly cemented by calcite to form a thin crust. Underneath the crust, as their horses' hooves broke through every now and then, Longarm glimpsed a richer, darker soil.

In the distance, paralleling their course, there were a few buttes, sheer, chimney-like affairs, volcanic plugs, as Longarm knew. Close to sundown, as they entered the valley Pettigrew had selected for his first dig, they found themselves riding quite close to one of the buttes they had seen before only at a great distance. It was an interesting landmark and it dominated the valley. Its sides were reddish in the setting sun and long, down-sweeping scour marks showed where rain and wind had sculpted its sides. On the top there were trees, and game trails crisscrossed its base.

Squinting up at it as they rode closer, Longarm glanced at Roberta. "Can you feel it?"

"Feel what?"

"The eyes watching?"

She frowned quickly at him. "Whose eyes?"

"Those of the watcher, a *mirador*—more than likely

from the top of that chimney of rock ahead of us."

"Are you sure?"

"The Indians and local Mexicans are. They always 'see' someone above them from the rims of canyons or buttes peering down at them. They take it rather calmly, considering."

"Who do they think is watching?"

Longarm said, "They just shrug and say *'Quien sabe?* They are always up there, watching.'"

"Could that be true?"

"Maybe. Could be goatherds or just Indians with nothing better to do. High places always attract people, don't they? There's something about climbing high and looking all over. I wouldn't think the Indians are any less likely to enjoy such a thing than we are."

"Yes," she said softly, glancing up at the top of the butte as they continued to draw closer to it. "I imagine you are right. I'd like to go up there if I could."

Longarm followed her gaze. "It would be a long climb for our horses, but it would be worth it."

They rode further on, silent, both of them thinking of the journey to the top of the butte as it grew larger and more massive with each passing second until they found that it blocked out most of the landscape ahead of them.

A quick pound of hoofbeats alerted Longarm. He turned to glance back and saw a very unhappy-looking Wynne Pettigrew lashing his horse to overtake them. Pulling alongside, his raw, sunburnt face doing little to hide the anger he felt, he fixed his mean eyes on Roberta. "I was wondering where you'd got off to!"

"Were you now?" Roberta answered lightly, the bare ghost of a smile on her face.

"Come with me!"

"Perhaps I prefer not to."

"Are we betrothed?"

"We are."

He halted his horse abruptly, cruelly. "Then come with me. We are about to camp. I have a few things I want to make clear!"

Roberta looked at Longarm, her dark eyes filled with deviltry. "I guess I have no choice, Longarm," she said. "My lord and master-to-be calls."

Longarm watched her ride off with Wynne, faintly amused. It was clear to him that Wynne Pettigrew was not going about things in the best way. Roberta Prescott was not a woman to be handled in this fashion.

Wynne was slighter in build than his brother Nathan. He was shorter, too, but with shoulders as broad as Longarm's. His hair was dark, closely cropped, his eyes were hazel, bright, feverish—and his actions just as feverish, it seemed. He was a young man in a hurry and everything he attempted was completed in a slipshod manner, with no care or pride. Longarm regarded him as a loose cannon, but his father apparently doted on him, while Nathan did his best to cover up his brother's mistakes and make excuses for him.

What Roberta saw in him mystified Longarm. But then, anything a beautiful woman did mystified him.

"We'll start digging here tomorrow," said Edward Pettigrew happily as he threw the dregs of his coffee into the fire.

"No, you won't," said Longarm.

"I beg your pardon, sir."

"You forgetting why I'm along? I'll be riding out

first thing in the morning to find the local chiefs in this valley. While I'm gone, if you stick the blade of a single shovel into this ground, I'll leave you to the Pimas and the Apaches."

"Why, sir, do you mean you'll abandon us to the aborigines!"

"Precisely."

"All of us—including Roberta?"

Longarm shrugged. "Look at it this way. If you people start digging up this sacred ground, I won't be any use to you. The Pimas won't listen to me then, and they'll likely show none of you any mercy at all."

Nathan spoke up abruptly. "All right, Longarm. Make your ride. Go find the chiefs. Bring them in and we'll parley."

Pettigrew's face reddened. "See here, son. Haven't you forgotten who's in charge of this expedition?"

"You are, Dad. But Longarm makes good sense. Start digging tomorrow morning and you'll have me to contend with."

"I never heard of such—"

"It's late, Dad," Nathan said wearily. "I suggest we all get some much needed sleep."

Longarm left for his soogan. He'd found a spot on a slight ridge above the campsite. As he climbed to it, he found himself pleased that Nathan was taking charge. He liked Nathan and had more respect for his good sense than for any one else on this dig—including his father.

He settled into his soogan, pulled the blanket over his shoulder, and closed his eyes. He was asleep almost instantly. A moment after, however, he was being shaken awake.

He opened his eyes. The moon was high, the stars overhead gleaming like diamonds cast upon velvet. But he didn't see much of the stars. Roberta was blocking his view, her long, magnificent hair enclosing his head and chest in a fragrant tent.

"What are you doing here?"

"I should think a man like you would know why I am here."

"You're engaged."

"Must I be punished, therefore?"

"I suppose not."

"Let me into that soogan," she said, lifting the tarp cover. "It's damn chilly out here with only this robe."

Longarm obliged on the instant, pushing back to give her room. As Roberta peeled out of her robe and snuggled under the covers close to him, he covered her and tried to clear his senses. He needed some information.

"What about you and Wynne?"

"I was a very bad girl. My brother wanted to become a member of Edward Pettigrew's prestigious expedition to the American Southwest in search of the fabled Hohokum. Since I knew that Wynne was interested in me, I let matters take their course—with the result that James is now a member of this expedition, and I am about to break a very foolish engagement."

"Poor Wynne."

"I gave him every chance to win me over, Longarm. But he is a priggish fool who has made me angry most of the time and in open revolt the rest of the time. Do you know what he said as we made camp?"

Remembering the way Wynne had come after Roberta, Longarm chuckled. "No, but I can guess."

"He forbade me to speak to you again."

19

"That is kind of silly of him."

"Silly? It's infuriating."

"Then you intend to keep on speaking to me?"

She smiled, snaked down with her hand, and found his rock-hard erection. "Yes," she said. "I most certainly do."

She kissed him then and Longarm parted his lips under the pressure of hers, and Roberta's tongue darted into his mouth. He found one of her breasts with his calloused hand and started to caress and squeeze it. Her lips parted more widely and the pressure of her hand squeezing on him became more insistent.

He shifted so he could look down at her, the tarp falling off his shoulders as he did so. The moon over his shoulder looked down just as eagerly as Longarm drank in the sight of the softly rounded curves of her pink-tipped breasts, the tautness of her abdomen, the gentle swelling of her stomach, and the dark, gleaming triangle at the apex of her thighs.

Longarm bent his head to rub his lips and the wiry hair of his longhorn mustache over the budded tips of her breasts, then pulled her to him. With a deep sigh, she opened her thighs and flung her arms about his neck, moving in under him smoothly.

"I'm more than ready for you, Longarm," she whispered huskily in his ear as she opened her thighs still wider and guided his massive erection. "I have been ready ever since I first saw you in the hotel room in Denver."

Longarm kissed her on the lips, then took his time, stealing in slowly until their two bodies were almost totally merged. Pausing for only an instant then, aware of her soft, delighted gasp, he drove the rest of the way

20

into her with a lunge that set her shuddering, her breath coming in short, ragged gasps.

"Don't move," she pleaded softly, her arms tightening around his neck. "Not for a while. I'm so close to letting go! And I don't want to—not yet."

Longarm lay still. He watched Roberta's face in the moon's dim light until her lips stopped twisting and settled into a relaxed smile. Then he began to stroke, gently and steadily.

Before long, unable to contain herself, Roberta exploded into a sudden frenzy of motion, twisting and heaving beneath him until he had to pin her with the full weight of his body. She continued to writhe beneath him until the breath rushed from her throat in a long, expiring moan. For a long while she lay in his arms, quivering, tiny beads of perspiration standing out on her forehead, her cheeks flushing to an amazing fullness. At last, one final gentle shudder passed through her long body, and she rested.

For several minutes she said nothing as she lay back remembering it, glorying in it. Then she looked at him.

"I disappointed you, didn't I?"

"Not for a minute," he assured her.

"But you didn't—"

"No. But there isn't any hurry."

"I tried to hold back. I really did. But that fool Wynne has no power to satisfy a woman, and he has been keeping me on a tight rein since we set out. And, like I said, I wanted you from the moment you stood up to face me in that hotel room."

"Well, you just got me."

"Yes. I just did. And you were all I imagined you would be."

21

"Thank you, ma'am."

"Here," she said excitedly. "We're not through yet." She grabbed him eagerly, and gasped, reaching up to fling both arms about his neck.

"Oh, that's it!" she cried. "Now drive on in! Deeper! Deeper! Let me take every inch of you!"

Longarm complied eagerly. Bracing his knees, he lunged forward, and kept thrusting, feeling himself building now, yet holding himself back until Roberta's throaty cries rose almost to a scream. He placed his big hand over her mouth so she wouldn't wake up the entire camp and felt the muscles of her stomach contracting convulsively under his muscular belly.

She shook off his hand and grinned up at him. "Now," she whispered hoarsely. "Now! Hurry, Longarm! Come when I do this time!"

He was way ahead of her. Letting himself go, he surged on, driving into her with two more violent thrusts. A second later he was shuddering violently in her grasp, draining himself completely in a long, sustained spasm that matched hers. He held himself pressed hard again her soft body, pulsing savagely, until at last she was through quivering. A sigh came from deep within her and she stirred as though to move away. He rolled gently off her.

Moaning contentedly, she stretched her strained legs out deep into the soogan, her eyes dreamy and half-shut. Longarm leaned over and kissed her gently on her eyelids. He enjoyed the quivering aliveness of them under his lips.

"Thank you, Longarm," Roberta whispered, kissing him softly on the lips. "It was worth it, coming here like this to your side. I knew you wouldn't fail me."

22

"You did me some good, too, don't forget."

"I sincerely hope so."

She reached for her robe and got up dazedly. He saw her stagger momentarily as she flung the robe over her shoulders. She blew some hair out of her eyes and smiled down at him. "Mmmm, I feel so good."

"Be careful," he told her. "You don't want Wynne to catch you."

"Oh, he knows I came up here to be with you. I told him. I don't like to go behind anyone's back."

With that, she waved and moved off down the slope, disappearing from sight a moment later. Longarm remained sitting up in his soogan, thinking over what she had just told him.

Then he shook his head and grinned. She was some woman, all right.

Longarm checked to make sure his Colt was under his pillow. It was. He released the safety catch, closed his eyes, and for the rest of that night slept like a contented baby.

Chapter 2

Bright and early the next morning, Longarm set out. He didn't have much doubt he would run into Pimas before long. They were probably already on his tail, he realized, as he glanced back up at the towering chimney of rock behind him. Maybe those *miradors* he had been discussing with Roberta were really Pimas keeping an eye on him.

Cresting a slight ridge, he mopped his brow and took out a cheroot. He promised himself he would not light it, just chew on it. Then he saw a small patch of dust—or was it smoke?—hanging in the air just above the distant horizon. Leaning forward in his creaking saddle, he thought he heard gunfire, very faint, and the sharp ki-yis of Indians attacking. It was dust *and* smoke he saw! Lifting the Winchester from his saddle sling, he spurred his horse on.

Distance in the desert is difficult to judge. It took Longarm almost an hour to reach the looted wagon and the two dead mules lying in its traces. He saw the last of the Indians riding off at his approach, but as he got to within a few hundred yards, a shot rang out from an outcropping of rocks just above the wagon and a round whispered a warning as it burned past his right ear.

He cantered back at least a hundred yards, then turned back around to peer up into the rocks. Taking off his hat, he waved it back and forth.

"Friend!" he called. *"Amigo!"*

Then he sat his horse, hunched down over his pommel, and waited.

After a few moments, he saw sunlight glinting off a rifle's breach, then a faint figure standing on one of the rocks. Longarm waved. The slim figure waved back.

Cautiously, Longarm urged his horse forward.

When he passed the burnt-out wagon, he saw the bodies of two Apaches hanging from the blackened tailgate. He kept going and, rounding a boulder, found three more dead Apaches. He glanced up in the rocks at the gent he had seen waving. He was clearly visible now, sitting with his chin cupped in his hands, his rifle leaning upright against a boulder beside him.

Dismounting at the foot of a rocky barrier, Longarm started up toward the fellow, still lugging his Winchester.

"You all right?" he yelled up.

"I'm fine!" came the high, thin response. "Just fine!"

The sarcasm was not lost on Longarm. He grinned and pulled himself higher. Beside him, a foot dislodged a small avalanche of gravel. Longarm turned to see an Apache coming for him, his long knife held high over his head. There was a hole in his chest, but it didn't seem to be slowing him down any. Longarm flung his Winchester around. The barrel slammed into the Indian's midsection. Longarm squeezed the trigger. The gun misfired. The Apache grabbed the barrel and flung it to one side. As Longarm reached across his belt buckle for his Colt, a shot from above shattered the Apache's skull.

As the Apache toppled down into the rocks below him, Longarm picked up his Winchester, checked the breach, then waved his thanks to the gent in the rocks above.

"Mebbe you better wait down there, mister," said the gent.

Longarm thought that was a fine idea, and picked his way back down to the desert floor. A moment later the rifleman scrambled down out of the rocks and joined him. Only it wasn't a rifleman. It was a girl with long dark hair woven into pigtails that hung down from her hatbrim, a full blossoming of womanhood pressing against her checked shirt, and large dark eyes that gleamed now with interest as they looked at Longarm. The bottom of her long dark skirt was torn and muddy, and her high-button boots were in bad shape.

"Thanks," she said.

"For what?"

"I knew that damned Apache was down there waiting for me. Didn't know where, though."

"I see. So you let me flush him for you."

"I had no other choice."

"I'm glad you're such a good shot. But why'd you shoot at me when I first rode up?"

"One of the Apaches in the wagon wasn't quite dead

27

yet. I saw him perking up as you rode closer."

"So you chased me back."

"Until the Apache lost his accursed spirit."

"What's your name?"

"Name's Charity. Charity Ryan," she said, thrusting out her tough little hand for him to shake. "What's yours?"

Longarm told her.

"Well, you are a big man, and that's a fact," she observed.

"What in blazes're you doing out here alone?"

She shrugged. "I was haulin' some goods from San Diego to Taos. Looks like they ain't goin' to get there. And I ain't got any more mules and no wagon to speak of. The rest of them redskin bastards took all my goods when they lit out."

"You were alone?"

"I hired a Mex to help out with the mules. He said he knew all about the danged brutes. He was a liar. He's back at the last water hole. That's where the Apaches found him."

"And you tried to run for it?"

"I made for these rocks. And I got here too—just in time."

Longarm glanced around him at the sprawled bodies. Usually Indians made a point of taking their dead with them. But Charity's fire had been too good for that, it appeared. "Looks like you accounted for quite a few."

"Not enough. Not near enough. I wish I'd gotten every damn one of the devils."

"Be satisfied. You still got your scalp."

"You got any idea what a scalp's worth in this empty land of sidewinders and scorpions? It won't buy me a single mule, never mind a new wagon."

He grinned. "Well, I might pay somethin' for them pigtails. Yes, I might at that."

"Now just what do you mean by that, mister?"

"Take your time and figure it out. Think maybe I'd go as high as a hundred dollars."

"Mighty white of you. Where you from, anyway?"

"Denver."

"That's a long way from here, ain't it? What're you doin' out here?"

"I'm with an archaeology expedition. I rode out this morning to find the local Pimas."

Charity's eyes caught something behind Longarm. Her face went suddenly hard. "You better forget about Pimas, mister. Here come those damn Apaches again. I sure hope you can fix that bum Winchester of yours."

Turning, Longarm studied the oncoming Indians, and after a moment he turned back to Charity with a relieved grin. "You can relax. They ain't Apaches. They're the Pima Indians I've been looking for."

Charity relaxed. "That's a help. They're friendlies, I been told."

"You been told right."

Holding his right palm out, Longarm left the rocks and walked out to meet the Pimas. There were five of them, riding stubby ponies. They had on war paint, but they seemed not at all warlike. As Longarm held up, expecting them to stop before him, they kept right on going past him. Not until they reached Charity did they pull their ponies to a halt and dismount.

As Longarm hurried after them, he saw the oldest of the Pimas, a chief by the look of his finery, raise his hand in greeting to Charity. Charity smiled at the old warrior and returned his greeting.

"You are mighty warrior. Kill many hated Apaches. I

call you Apache Killer. You are welcome in the Pima nation. Forever!"

Charity's dark eyes sparkled. "Hey, I really appreciate that, Chief. Thanks a lot."

Only then did the five Pimas turn their attention to Longarm. The chief fixed Longarm with his cold, black eyes. Almost as tall as Longarm, his cheekbones were prominent, his jaw solid, his face furrowed with deep wrinkles.

"You," the chief said, pointing a long, powerful finger at Longarm. "Who are you?"

"I am Longarm to my friends."

"I am Tall Coyote, chief of the Pimas." He strode closer to Longarm, peering at him intently. "Longarm, what you want in this land? You lead many into valley of our forefathers. Why you do this thing? It is not what we want."

"I been searching for you, Chief. I'd like you to come with me and let the gents I'm with explain what they have in mind."

"Is no gold in this valley!"

"It ain't gold we're after."

"Then what is it you seek? The bite of the scorpion?"

"Not that either, Chief."

Tall Coyote pulled from his saddle pouch a pair of army binoculars. Flourishing them, he said, "With these long eyes Tall Coyote see you come into his valley with your people—and he watch you leave them and ride through valley. Then I see you help Apache Killer and kill Apache. So Tall Coyote will be friend of Longarm. He will go back with him to the camp of his people. But he make no promise and he will sign no treaty."

"It's a deal, Chief. No treaties, no promises."

Longarm was satisfied. He had ridden out that morn-

30

ing in search of one of Pima chiefs, and the chief had found him. The fact that Longarm would also be bringing in a dark-eyed Apache killer in skirts just made the cheese more binding.

Longarm turned to Charity. "You'll have to ride up behind me. Think you can manage that?"

"Sure," she said. Then she smiled.

Longarm grinned back at her. The real question was, could *he* manage it?

It was close to sundown when Longarm rode into camp with Charity and the Pima Indians. At sight of the Pima warriors, the digger Indians promptly vanished into the desert. Not one of them looked back. Furious at this desertion, Pettigrew puffed himself up to his full height as Longarm dismounted and helped Charity down.

"And just who is this young lady, Longarm?" .

"Charity Ryan. And any more explanations about her can wait. This here's a Pima chief, and five of his trusted warriors. Name's Tall Coyote."

"I must say I am not happy at you bringing these aborigines into our camp without warning. As you can see, they have driven off our porters. I doubt if we'll see a single one of them again."

"Look at it this way, Pettigrew: you won't have much need for them if you don't convince Chief Tall Coyote that your digging in his people's ground will not upset the valley's spirit population."

Pettigrew frowned. "Spirit population? Oh, I see. Of course. All right," he snapped. "I'll speak to him. But he'll have to dismount. I am not going to walk over there and look up at him like some damned penitent. You tell him that."

"Dismount, Chief," Longarm called out to Tall

31

Coyote. "You are welcome in our camp!"

Pettigrew was upset. "I didn't say that!"

"No, but you damn well should have," Longarm snapped angrily.

Roberta had already hurried out of the darkness to greet Charity. After a brief, friendly exchange, the two hurried off, while Nathan and the other young men flanked Pettigrew as the expedition's director folded his arms imperiously and waited for Tall Coyote to approach. Pettigrew uttered not a single word of welcome as the Pima chief neared him.

This did not go unnoticed. Pulling up a few feet from Pettigrew, Tall Coyote glanced at Longarm. "I do not like this chief of yours," he told Longarm. "He is proud enough, but he has no sense. And he has no manners. He is on my people's sacred land, yet he thinks he owns it."

Pettigrew's face reddened in indignation. He had puffed himself up to await the Pima chief's approach and now he looked ready to burst. Watching him, Longarm wondered how much longer this expedition could survive with such a pompous ass in charge.

"Now, see here, Chief," Pettigrew protested. "My manners are certainly the equal of any stone-age aborigine's. You have ridden here uninvited. And now you tell me this is your people's land. This land belongs to the United States of America. It is being administered by the Bureau of Indian Affairs in Washington. So let's not hear any more about whose land this is."

"I piss on the Bureau of Indian Affairs," Tall Coyote said. "Do you not have lodge where we can smoke pipe?"

"Pipe? Sir, I do not smoke. I consider it a vile habit. Nor do I chew."

32

"He don't drink, neither," drawled Longarm, winking at the chief.

Fortunately, this remark broke some of the tension. Tall Coyote glanced at Longarm and smiled, showing a prominent gold tooth. "This man is fool. He is not chief. I will not talk with him," he announced grandly. "I will talk with Longarm, the killer of Apaches."

Longarm looked over at Pettigrew. "You heard the chief, Pettigrew. Go over to your tent and sulk like a good boy. The rest of you can go with him. Me and the chief'll find a spot to parley."

Shocked, Pettigrew started to bluster, but Nathan took his arm and led him away with the other two men. Longarm indicated with a sweep of his hand that the other five Pima Indians could dismount if they wished. They immediately slipped off their ponies and squatted in a circle.

A moment later Longarm found a spot close to where he had slept the previous night, and providing a blanket for himself and the chief, sat down cross-legged. Not having a pipe, Longarm gave the chief one of his cheroots, which he liked instantly.

After they had both lit up and puffed a while in contented silence, the chief tipped his head slightly and said, "This man Pettigrew is from the East."

"Yes."

"He has no sense."

"Yes."

"Then what does he want here in this valley?" the chief asked.

"He wants to dig—but not for gold."

"Then why does he dig?"

"He seeks those things the Hohokum have left behind. He feels the Hohokum are a great people, too

33

great to be the Pima's ancestors. He thinks they came from a far, distant land. And that they went back to that land to let the desert claim this valley once more."

"He is a fool. The Hohokum are our ancestors!"

"Perhaps so, but this man does not think so."

Tall Coyote shrugged. "It is as I told you. He has no sense."

"That may be. But many in the East think he is very wise. They listen to him and they nod their heads in agreement. Soon the world will agree with him. The Pima will be an orphan people, stripped of their rightful ancestors. There will be no reason then to protect this land."

Tall Coyote's eyes narrowed shrewdly. "Then will come railroad?"

"Or worse."

"What could be worse?"

"A dam."

"Ah!" Tall Coyote knew at once just how much worse that would be. The Indian had already seen much land vanish under the white man's mania for dam building in order to create reservoirs for its rapidly growing cities.

"It is hard," Tall Coyote said, shaking his head sadly.

"What is hard, Chief?"

"To see what you white eyes do to the land of our forefathers. I think you want only to flood the land, cut down the trees, and rip up the grasslands with your plows. If you have your way, you will turn the land to stone. No elk, no antelope, no bears will survive. Only the rats that follow you will prosper and multiply. I have but a few years left. I will not see it. But it makes me sad, even so."

"It is a sickness we have," Longarm agreed. "We call it civilization. Now, will you let this fool dig in the ground?"

"Will he find the truth about our ancestors?"

"Yes."

"And then will he admit my people are the true descendants of the Hohokum? Will he admit our land is sacred to us, that the desert spirits must be allowed to sleep in peace?"

"If he finds no proof the Hohokum came from a distant continent and returned to it, Pettigrew will make this known to all. There will no longer be any reason for digging up your valley."

"And there will not come again other white eyes with shovels and digger slaves?"

"Chief, I have no magic for looking into the future. I am like you. I never know what the white eyes will do next."

Tall Coyote nodded sagely, obviously impressed by Longarm's candor. "Since the first white man came to this land," he said musingly, "the People have not raised their hand to them. When the white eyes fight the Apache, the People help them. Even now we have many scouts in the army to seek out and kill the hated Apache. I think I will believe you, Longarm. But keep that foolish Pettigrew away from me. And, remember, I will sign no treaties."

"Then you will let Pettigrew dig."

"Yes. But he can dig only where he is now. If he takes his shovels and digs anywhere he want, I say no."

"Agreed."

Longarm passed four cheroots across to Tall Coyote. The chief took them gratefully. The meeting was over.

Pettigrew could begin his dig—as long as he stayed where he was.

The next morning, after Longarm had again spelled out the limits of the agreement with Tall Coyote to the disgruntled Pettigrew, Longarm and Charity left the dig and headed for Lizard Gulch, so she could get a train for Taos. Once they were out of sight of the dig, Charity nudged the horse Roberta had loaned her up alongside Longarm.

She glanced mischievously at Longarm. "Roberta told me a lot about you."

Longarm shrugged.

"She says you're as much a man out of the saddle as in it."

Longarm glanced at her. "We better keep our eyes open, Charity. Them Apaches who cleaned you out may be anxious to fix you good and proper."

"Fix both of us maybe."

"Yep."

"You figure them Apaches're still around?"

"I wouldn't put it past them."

"You're hopin' the Pimas can keep the Apaches away from the dig?"

"I'm sure of it. Otherwise, I wouldn't be escorting you to Lizard Gulch."

"You'd let me go alone, you mean."

"I mean I'd keep you at the dig until we all went back."

Charity nodded, satisfied. During the rest of the ride to Lizard Gulch, she decided to tell him about herself. She was the daughter of a forty-niner and a dance-hall girl. Her father died of alcoholism and her mother died of tuberculosis soon after his death. Charity was twelve at the time. She married a traveling salesman when she was fourteen, left him and married a saloon owner when she was nineteen. He was a mean brute who got shot in an altercation with a drunken customer, and since then, she was proud to say, she had kept herself out of the marriage pen. That didn't mean she didn't enjoy a man's company now and then, she told Longarm hopefully. She just didn't see why it always had to lead to wedding bells.

It was close to sunset and they were within sight of Lizard Gulch. Longarm glanced at her. "Well, Charity, maybe you're a mite too young for marriage anyway. How old are you?"

"Gettin' pretty old," she admitted gloomily. "I'm twenty-two."

"Well, maybe you'll meet some nice gent one of these days and settle down."

"I'm lookin' at one setch gentleman right now," she said, grinning at him impishly.

"You're too young. I'm too old."

"You're never too old, Longarm. Besides, old bulls like to feed on fresh grass."

Ignoring her drift, Longarm asked if she had any kin that she knew of in Taos, and she admitted she had.

"Name's Tanner Ryan," she said. "My pa's brother. Runs a saddle shop. I was figurin' on visitin' him when I got there with them goods."

By that time they were moving down Lizard Gulch's wide, dusty main street, heading for the train depot's water tower on the far side of town. When they reached the depot, Longarm escorted Charity inside and bought her a ticket for Taos. Then he sent a telegram to Billy

Vail, telling him all was going smoothly so far. He didn't think there was any reason to mention Apaches, or the dust that had been trailing them for the past two hours.

Outside, fingering her ticket, Charity was waiting for him. "This here's real generous of you, Longarm."

"Forget it."

"Thing is, we make such a great team."

"Team?"

"Killin' Apaches, I mean."

"Oh."

"Seems silly to break up such a good team. Don't you think?"

"I can't make you my deputy, Charity. You'd best go on to Taos, where you were heading anyway."

"I ain't got nothin' to bring to Taos now."

"I'm sure your Uncle Ryan will be pleased to see you."

"You wouldn't be tryin' to get rid of me, would you?"

"Charity, you got your business and I got mine."

"You mean those crazy dudes out there in the desert, digging for bones and old pots."

He sighed. "That's my business, all right."

"This here train won't be gettin' here till tomorrow mornin', late. I guess I'll have to stay here overnight. You anxious to ride back to them dudes, are you?"

"Not particularly."

"So let's eat sittin' on chairs and maybe get some shuteye above the ground for a change."

He looked down at her and grinned. "Ain't such a bad idea, at that."

* * *

The only hotel in town turned out to have a decent dining room. They ate their late supper in the nearly empty dining room, by a front window that enabled them to look out at the wide street. The town had not yet installed gas lamps, so the only light came from the moon overhead and from the two taverns bracketing the hotel. A lamp hanging above the livery's wide-open stable door spilled additional light out onto the street.

It was just enough for Longarm to see a shadowy figure peering out through the livery's entrance. A pale headband held back his black, shoulder-length hair. Then down the middle of the street rode an Apache, his lance tip gleaming in the moonlight, his glance darting from right to left as he rode. Behind him came four other mounted Apaches. Up the street a townsman appeared on a porch and raised a rifle. A shadow came to life behind him and Longarm saw the man yanked swiftly back into the Apache's blade. The townsman died without an outcry.

"My God!" gasped Charity as she saw the lead Apache riding past the hotel.

"Recognize him?"

"He's the leader of the band that attacked my wagon!"

"Then I guess maybe we know who he's lookin' for."

There was a slight commotion from the restaurant's kitchen. Longarm swiftly blew out the lantern on his table, grabbed Charity, and flung her to the ground just as two Apaches slipped through the kitchen doorway into the dining room.

A man and a woman were dining in a far corner. The woman let out a scream. The first Apache turned and fired his rifle at her, levered quickly, and fired at her dinner companion. Amidst a clatter of silverware and broken china, the two collapsed to the floor. By this time Longarm unholstered his .44. He aimed it at the Apache and blew his head off. The second Apache ducked to the floor. Then, using the tables and chairs for cover, he started for Longarm.

"Keep back," Longarm whispered to Charity.

She nodded.

Longarm moved out and away from the table to draw fire from Charity. He caught a glimpse of the Apache's head and fired quickly. The bullet glanced off a table and slammed into the wall behind the Apache. Crabbing sideways, he ducked behind the corner of the bar, near the entrance to the dining room.

The Apache suddenly stood boldly up and sent a rapid fusillade at the spot where Longarm had been a second before. Longarm stepped out from behind the bar and fired twice into the Apache's chest. The Apache crumpled.

"Look out!" Charity cried.

She jumped up from behind their table and flung herself at Longarm, slamming him back against the bar. As she did so, two Apaches appeared in the dining room doorway. One loosed a hatchet at Longarm, the other fired his rifle at him. The hatchet missed, but the Apache rifleman caught Charity square in the back. The bullet ranged up through it, exited, and slammed into the bar beside Longarm.

He spun and emptied his .44 into the two Indians.

As they staggered back, dead on their feet, a third Apache raced into the hotel lobby. It was the chief. Longarm flung his empty revolver at the Apache, then ducked back into the dining room and sought shelter behind an overturned table along the far wall. Assuming Longarm had no weapon, the Apache kicked aside Charity's limp body and strode swiftly into the room after Longarm.

Longarm took his derringer from his vest pocket and released the safety. The Apache loomed close. Flinging aside the table behind which Longarm was crouching, the Apache raised his lance. Longarm emptied both barrels into the Apache's face. The Apache dropped his lance and collapsed back, coming to rest between two overturned tables.

Pushing past the dead Indian and ignoring the sudden crowd of gun-toting citizens racing into the hotel's dining room, Longarm bent over Charity's seemingly lifeless form. Cradling her head in his arms, he leaned close to her.

"Charity! Can you hear me?"

Her eyes opened. "They didn't get you, Longarm?"

"No, Charity, they didn't."

"I'm hurt bad, ain't I?"

"You took a slug in the back, but the bullet went on through."

"Feels like it's still sitting there," she gasped.

Longarm glanced up at the gaping faces peering down. "You got a doctor in this town?"

"Sure, Doc Winslow."

"Get him!"

As the fellow who had answered turned and ran from the place, Longarm picked Charity up and carried her out of the dining room. They had taken a room before dining. Longarm carried Charity up the stairs and into the room. The desk clerk and the hotel manager followed him in. The desk clerk closed the door behind him while the manager pulled down the covers, then lit the kerosene lamp on the dresser.

Longarm deposited Charity's limp, bleeding form on the clean sheets. He felt like crying. Charity opened her eyes and looked at him. "I told you," she said.

"Told me what?"

"That we made a nice team."

"Some team. I let you take a bullet meant for me."

"You didn't have anything to say about it."

Just then the doctor barged in, a round elderly Indian woman with him. Doc Winslow shooed everyone out of the room, including Longarm.

Before going back down the stairs, Longarm reloaded his Colt and the derringer.

In front of the hotel a large crowd was milling. Everyone was shouting at once. A few carried torches. Rifle and gun barrels gleamed in every hand. From the excited townsmen Longarm learned there were at least two Apaches still loose in the town.

Someone ran up. "I saw them!" he cried.

"Where?" Longarm demanded.

"In the back alley across the street. They ducked into the livery!"

Longarm darted across the street to the livery entrance. Out of the shadows beside it, a bewhiskered old-timer materialized, a plains rifle in his hand.

"This's my livery, stranger," he told Longarm. "And I aim to make sure these bastards don't burn it down. You neither."

"You want me to flush these Apaches, or don't you?"

"Why you so all-fired eager to get your head blown off?"

"Let's just say I got some incentive."

The old-timer spat a dark streak of chewing tobacco and said, "All right. Let's go. I'll cover you."

Longarm eased himself into the stable. Off to his right, some horses were stamping nervously. He pointed his Colt in that direction, then followed its lead toward that corner of the stable.

After he was well inside the stable, he heard someone drop from the loft to the floor behind him. He whirled in time to accept a dagger's blade in his chest. As the blade plunged home, Longarm staggered back, amazed, then wrested the knife from the Apache's hand and clubbed him to the floor of the livery with his Colt.

Another Apache loomed out of a stall, a lance in his hand. Longarm turned to face him, but he was no longer as swift as he needed to be. Just as the Apache lunged, the old-timer's plains rifle rang out. The impact of the round was powerful enough to spin the Apache around and slam him back into a pile of horse dung.

"Thanks, mister," Longarm said to the old-timer as he shifted his Colt to his left hand and held his right hand over his gouting wound.

"Sorry I didn't catch that other bastard," the fellow replied, peering close at Longarm's wound. In the near blackness of the livery stable, neither man could see the wound very clearly, but Longarm knew for sure that he was losing a hell of a lot of blood.

From the street outside came shouts as the townsmen flocked across the street to the livery's entrance, now that the last Apaches had been accounted for.

"How many did you see enter the stable?" Longarm asked the old-timer.

"Can't say."

"I heard two."

"That's what I heard," said the liveryman.

"Well, actually, there were three."

"Three?"

"Yes," Longarm said, raising the Colt and firing at the Apache who had just stepped from a stall. The Apache dropped his bow. The arrow he had been drawing back slammed into the livery floor, and as the Apache fell forward he impaled himself on the feathered end of his shaft.

"Help me out of here," said a woozy Longarm. "I think I need to see that doctor who's upstairs with the girl."

As the two men emerged from the stable, a cheer rose from the relieved townsmen. Longarm barely heard it; he was too weak by this time to hear much of anything. And his chest hurt bloody awful.

"Hey! Look out!" a townsman cried. "There's another Apache!"

The man flung up his double-barrel shotgun and let loose into the stable. At once those around him went to their knees in a panic and began emptying their revolvers into the livery.

Just inside the doorway, two horses slumped to the floor of the livery, whinnying and kicking frantically.

"Hold off!" cried the old-timer. "Them ain't Apaches! Them's my horses!"

Sheepishly, the men holstered their weapons, but the damage had been done. A thick plume of smoke began to pulse out through the door. The hay in the loft had been ignited when the fusillade of bullets hit the kerosene in the livery's lamps.

"Get the other horses!" someone shouted.

As some men formed a bucket brigade, others rushed into the barn to free the horses. Longarm started back through the crowd. When he reached the hotel, his shirtfront and pants were covered with blood. Two men saw his condition and helped him up to his room. Inside it, Charity was resting comfortably in the bed and Doc Winslow was packing his black bag.

When the doctor saw Longarm's bloody figure collapsing into a chair, he reopened his bag without a word and bent to examine him. That was all Longarm remembered.

When he awoke, he found his chest wound closed and bandaged, the sun streaming through the window, and Charity sitting up in a rocker, a blanket thrown over her lap.

"Hi, lazybones," she said.

He waved his hand at her and tried to speak. He found he could barely utter a sound, and when he tried to speak up, his right lung protested alarmingly.

"Guess I'll just have to whisper," he said to her.

"The doc said you got a punctured lung. But he thinks you'll be all right."

"What about you?"

"I'll be fit as a fiddle in no time."

"How long have we been laid up?"

"Almost a week."

Longarm could hardly believe it. He thought at once of the expedition's members back in the desert valley, waiting for him. By this time they must have realized he had run into trouble. They might even have concluded he was dead, in which case Pettigrew might decide he was no longer bound by Longarm's agreement with the Pimas to dig only where Longarm and Tall Coyote had designated.

That could mean trouble.

Goaded by this thought, Longarm decided to get up and get the hell out of there. He pushed himself upright, but could not make it any further. He had all the strength of a wet dishtowel. With a weary sigh, he leaned back. Smiling, Charity got up and walked carefully over to the bed. Throwing back his covers, she got in beside him.

"Don't worry," she told him. "I locked the door when I saw you coming to your senses."

"You must be crazy. I'm in no condition."

"Shush. Who do you think I been sleeping with this past week?"

"Well, it couldn't have done you much good."

"It was nice. You snore sometimes and you cry out some in your dreams. But it was better than nothing. Now lie still and let me put my arms around you. It won't hurt, and it just might do you some good."

Longarm didn't argue. A few minutes later, enclosed in her arms, he dropped off into a deep, peaceful sleep.

As soon as the train came into view, Charity turned to look up at Longarm. Her face was understandably pale from her long convalescence, and she appeared considerably more of a lady than when she had ridden into Lizard Gulch with Longarm almost two weeks before. Her hair was in a bun piled up under her blue bonnet, the bonnet's strings tied neatly beneath her chin. Her long, lovely neck was protected by a filigree of lace, and her severe, tight-fitting bottle-green jacket effectively hid the rising beauties Longarm had spent so many delightful hours exploring, while her dark blue silk skirt covered her legs clear to the tops of her high-button shoes.

46

"I don't want to go, Longarm," she said.

"Think of your uncle. He's answered both of my telegrams. He'll be looking for you. You'll have a family again, Charity."

"But we made such a good team, you and I."

"That we did."

"All right. I'll go on to Taos, but if it don't work out, I'm comin' back. Hell, Longarm, between the two of us we maybe could wipe out the whole Apache nation."

"That's a rather grisly ambition, ain't it, Charity?"

"Well, then, we can wear out every hotel bed in the territory."

He laughed.

The train pulled to a halt, escaping steam brushing across the platform. A conductor swung down, put down the steps, and helped Charity up into the coach. Longarm followed after her, carrying her luggage. She found a seat. He placed her valise on the rack over it.

She reached up. He took her hand, bent and kissed her on the lips. When he straightened, he saw tears on Charity's lightly freckled face. He dared not say a thing. He touched the brim of his hat to her, turned, and fled the train.

A moment later, as the train pulled out and he waved goodbye to Charity, he knew he would never see her again. Nothing was as easily torn as a woman's heart, and none of God's creatures could recover as completely or as quickly. He watched the train chuff off under its cloud of black smoke, then went into the train station to telegraph Vail and let him know that he was well enough to ride again and was on his way out to the dig.

The telegram sent, he stepped back out into the cruel sunshine, fixed his snuff-brown Stetson on carefully, and reached for a cheroot. As he did so, he caught sight of two dim figures half a mile down the track, hurrying across into a clump of scrub cactus. They were leading two very sorry-looking horses. But even at that distance, and despite the shimmering heat waves that rose from the hot ground between them, Longarm recognized them.

Chapter 3

About three miles out of Lizard Gulch, Longarm
glanced along the horizon and caught the glint of sunlight on sabers. Peering more closely, he saw the shimmering figures of the cavalry, and behind the column a
long, low cloud of dust. Troopers. Since they were
heading straight for him, he turned his mount slightly
and headed toward a small butte, its steep flanks clothed
with shrubbery. Dismounting, he found a small stream,
watered his horse, and then drank deep himself. Then
he hunkered down to wait for the army.

When the soldiers reached him about half an hour
later, a weary, dust-covered lieutenant dismounted.
Longarm stood up. The lieutenant, a young fellow just
out of West Point from the look of him, walked up to
Longarm and saluted.

"There's enough shade and water for your entire

company, Lieutenant," Longarm told the youngster. "Why not let them light and rest a spell."

The lieutenant took out his handkerchief, mopped his grimy brow, then waved his men off their mounts. That was when Longarm saw the three men leading a mule team. Shovels and pickaxes were sticking out of the packs.

"I am Lieutenant Carswell, sir," the lieutenant said. "Whom do I have the honor of addressing?"

"Name's Custis Long," Longarm replied, shaking the young soldier's hand. "But it won't be much of an honor, I'm afraid. I'm a deputy U. S. marshal. Mind telling me what you and your men're doing out here?"

The lieutenant grinned. "Believe it or not, Mr. Long, I am in search of a team of eastern archaeologists. They are supposed to be digging up the desert out here somewhere, looking for bones and other remains. These three scientists with me are to join this expedition."

Longarm glanced back at the three archaeologists. "They're extra special, are they?"

The lieutenant nodded firmly.

"Who's the big man in Washington backing them?"

"Senator Bradish from Connecticut. These scientists are from the museum at Yale. It seems they are supposed to be digging in place of that other group already here. I don't understand it too clearly myself, but it seems the Yale museum is some sort of a rival to the Smithsonian."

"Don't try to understand it, Lieutenant. I've seen this sort of thing before. There's no way to make it any clearer than it already is. Anyway, you're in luck. I'm with that dig you mentioned, and I'm on my way back to them right now. You leave these three with me and

I'll escort them the rest of the way."

"That's decent of you, Deputy Long, but I have my orders. There's a renegade Apache band operating in the vicinity. A mean bunch, from what I hear."

"You got any kind of description of their leader?"

"I have."

"Let's have it."

The lieutenant described a tall, wiry-looking Apache who matched perfectly the description of the Apache chief into whose face Longarm had emptied his derringer.

"You can forget about them, Lieutenant," Longarm told him. "They rode into Lizard Gulch a couple of weeks ago and never rode out again."

"You want to explain that?"

Longarm explained it.

"Well," the lieutenant exclaimed mildly when Longarm had finished. "That's some story. I am sure the captain will be glad to hear this."

"I'm sure he will."

Longarm left the lieutenant so the lieutenant could water his horse and see to his own needs while Longarm strolled over to the three scientists from Yale. As he approached them, Longarm found he was not at all impressed. After introducing himself to the three, he inquired if any of them knew Edward Pettigrew, the leader of the Smithsonian expedition.

"I have heard of him," said Percival Gladstone, the leader of this small group, "but I have never met him."

Gladstone was a small, knobby fellow wearing glasses so thick the sun was apt to burn a hole in his cheek if he were not careful. Despite the heat he was wearing a tweed suit and vest over a heavy cotton shirt and low-cut shoes. His nose was burned almost cherry red by the sun, and his tweed hat had only a narrow brim, giving him very little protection from the sun.

"Maybe when you meet, you can both work together in the dig," Longarm suggested.

"Work together?"

"Yes."

"I don't think you understand. There is no room for any other archaeologists at this site. And Yale has priority. I have a letter from Senator Bradish and the president of Yale himself."

"*I* don't think *you* understand, Mr. Gladstone. I've spoken to the Pima Indians. They have allowed Pettigrew to excavate at the spot where he is now working. These Indians don't know you. So you'll either join with Pettigrew at this same dig or make your own deal with the Pimas."

"Then we shall do that."

"Suit yourself."

Longarm glanced at Gladstone's assistants. Again, he wasn't very impressed. One was quite frail looking. Despite the sun and the blistering heat, he looked as pale as a bedsheet, clammy almost. His Adam's apple bulged and his eyes bugged slightly. He looked away nervously when Longarm peered at him.

Gladstone saw Longarm looking at his two assistants and remembered his manners. "Forgive me, Mr. Long," he said coldly. "This here is Irving Smithers." He indicated the thin, pale fellow. "And next to him is my assistant, Keith Masters."

Longarm nodded to both men, since neither seemed anxious to shake his hand. Keith Masters was a slovenly fellow, dressed for the country, with a patched, wide-brim hat and a stomach that flowed well out over his belly. Strapped around his waist was a gunbelt, a Smith and Wesson stuck into the holster. He sure as hell was a queer-looking assistant for a snooty archaeologist from Yale.

Longarm left Gladstone and returned to his horse.

When Longarm rode into the dig late the next day, Nathan and Roberta seemed quite glad to see him and hurried over as he dismounted, while Edward Pettigrew acknowledged his return with only a grim nod. Without waiting for introductions from Longarm, he strode over to meet the lieutenant. Wynne and James Prescott went with him.

"How're things going?" Longarm asked Nathan and Roberta, his eyes sweeping the dig. He noticed a crude wall emerging from the ground where they had carted away the topmost layer of sand. The wall looked old enough, but not as old as Longarm would have expected.

"We've uncovered a rich site," said Nathan eagerly. "We already have some pottery."

"That's nice. How much do you think you can get for it?"

Roberta laughed. "Not much, I'm thinking. What kept you, Longarm? We thought maybe you'd given up on us and gone back to Denver."

"Met them same Apaches that attacked Charity, in Lizard Gulch this time. Got myself and Charity banged up some. That's all."

"And Charity?"

"She's on her way to Taos."

"How'd you manage that, Longarm?" Nathan asked,

a mischievous gleam in his eye.

"It took some doing," Longarm admitted, cheerfully enough.

"We've been working hard, too," said Roberta. "Who're the three men with the cavalry?"

"Rivals from Yale. They want to dig here too, looks like."

"From Yale?" Nathan exploded, incredulous. "That's impossible."

"Maybe so. But they got letters from the president of Yale and from a Connecticut senator."

"Bradish?"

"That's the one."

"What's the lieutenant's name?" Roberta asked, shading her eyes as she looked him over while he spoke to Edward Pettigrew.

"Lieutenant Carswell. Fresh out of West Point, seems like."

"Dad is not going to like to share this dig, Longarm, and certainly not with anyone from Yale," Nathan said.

"He'll have to. I don't think I can get Tall Coyote to give us any more land to dig on. He'll see the handwriting on the wall then. Me, too."

Roberta nodded glumly. "I know what you mean. How many teams of archaeologists can this valley handle?"

The three of them walked over to join the discussion that was now heating up around the lieutenant.

It was night. Lieutenant Carswell had long since ridden off. Gladstone and his two men sat around one fire, Pettigrew and his people around another. A few minutes before, Longarm had retreated to his ridge above the dig. Now, squatting down and puffing on his cheroot, he looked down at the divided camp and grinned. They were like little boys playing fool games, but they sure as hell took themselves seriously.

He heard the rattle of sand, then a pebble bouncing off the edge of the ridge. His Colt in his hand, Longarm turned. Roberta loomed out of the night, saw the yawning muzzle of Longarm's Colt, and gasped.

Longarm holstered the gun and grinned at Roberta. She was wearing only the flimsiest of nightgowns. It buttoned up the front, but she hadn't bothered to button much of it. One breast was nearly uncovered and glowed softly in the moon's luminous light. He wanted to reach up and take it in both his hands, but he kept himself in check.

"I was expecting someone else," he explained.

"My God, who?"

"A crazy old lady and her son—the two Nathan and his father helped escape in Denver."

"You mean they're out here?"

"It could have been that I was seeing things, I suppose."

Roberta shuddered as she sat down beside him. Longarm put his arm around her. "That's better," she said. "Much better."

"Have you made up with Wynne?"

"The engagement's off."

"What about Nathan?"

"He's too much under his father's thumb. But I like him a lot better than Wynne."

"Me, too."

"Longarm, I'm worried," Roberta told him.

"Why?"

"You say those Pima Indians are friendly—that they'll do what their chief tells them?"

"I said they were friendly. But I never said they would do what their chief tells them."

"I don't understand. You made an agreement with the chief."

"Yes, I did. And if the rest of the band decides to go along with the chief, there'll be no problem. But no member of any band feels personally bound by the word of a chief. He can go his own way whenever he wants—and so can the rest of the band, for that matter."

"But that's anarchy!"

"No, it's individuality. Real individuality. Indians are very democratic. Each brave is free to go his own way. A chief governs only by example and prestige. He has no other power. He cannot *make* any brave follow him, and the moment he tells his people to do what they don't want to do, he is no longer chief."

"Then if any of Tall Coyote's band want to drive us out of this valley, they can?"

"True enough. First they will have to deal with Tall Coyote, however."

"Then Tall Coyote cannot protect us if the rest of his band refuses to go along with him?"

"There's nothing he can do."

"Now I'm really worried."

"Why? I've spoken to Tall Coyote. He seems to be in complete control of his band. There's no danger."

"Maybe there is. Maybe the chief is not in control."

"Why do you think that?"

"While you were gone, we were visited by the Pimas. Tall Coyote was not with them. Each time, they asked about you. Two days ago they came again and when they found you had not yet returned, they grew quite bold. One of them dismounted and approached me. He seemed interested in me, Longarm. Very interested." She shuddered.

He drew her closer to comfort her, but he didn't like what he had just heard.

"Well, I'm back now," he told her. "I'll go find Tall Coyote and remind him of our deal. And at the same time, it might be wise for me to explain these three newcomers."

"They don't impress me, Longarm."

"Me neither."

"I should think Yale could do better."

"Not to mention Senator Bradish."

"Let me go with you."

"You'll be safer here."

She thought that over for a while. "I suppose so, but it won't be nearly as much fun."

She reached down and unbuckled his gunbelt, then slipped his vest off his shoulders and began to unbutton his shirt. He kicked off his boots and peeled down his pants. She flung off her nightgown and pressed him down beneath her, laughing softly. Then she kissed him, long and hard. He felt himself growing like an eager plant in the sunlight, thrusting up through her legs.

She chuckled and leaned back, her hand knifing down so she could guide him into her. Then she sat back. He felt himself plowing deep within her and then heard her sigh as she leaned all the way back and sucked him deep up into her. Her muscle control was astounding. It was as if her hand was closing about his throbbing shaft.

He gasped out his pleasure.

57

She laughed. "It feels so good," she told him in a husky whisper, "to have something so nice and big to wrap around—to really get a firm grip on."

"Pleased to oblige."

He reached up and caressed her breasts. Her nipples sprang up to his touch; his hands explored further, reveling in the soft, silken warmth of her breasts. She began rising and falling, while she leaned forward on her hands so he could take her breasts in his mouth.

She cried out in delight as his tongue flicked over and around her nipples, turning them to hard fire. He heard her mutter, then shriek softly. With his mouth devouring her breasts, he reached down and began slamming her down repeatedly onto his shaft. It was on fire. He lifted himself and her high, then crashed her down upon him recklessly.

"Yes! Yes! Yes! Yes . . . !" she hissed. "Don't stop!"

Twice more he slammed her down onto his engorged shaft. Then his groin erupted and he exploded inside her. It was like a cannon going off. She took it all, letting out a delighted squeal as she felt his ejaculation pouring into her. She clung to him eagerly, then suddenly leaned all the way back, her face taut and covered with perspiration as she began to come herself. Once was not enough for her as she began to shudder in a series of tiny explosions.

Looking up, watching the flush creep across her face, he began to grow again inside her. She laughed as she felt him filling her once more and kept coming, leaning back with her back arched, her head thrown back, enjoying it with her eyes closed serenely and a pleased little smile on her face.

By the time she finished climaxing, she had him hot

again. He pulled her swiftly under him, nudged her thighs apart, and drove deep into her. His urgency delighted her. She locked her legs around his waist, then flung her arms around his neck and kissed him, her mouth opening, her tongue darting deep. Longarm found himself banging away without finesse or consideration—and already more than halfway there.

Roberta hung on, delighted, her tongue still grappling with his. Then she gasped, her hands tightening around his neck. He pulled his mouth away from hers, slammed home twice more, and exploded. Then she too came alive, pulsing happily beneath him, her eyes closed, her lips parted slightly as she savored every involuntary shudder as she—like him—came again and again.

At last they were both quiet in each other's arms. To his surprise, he found himself stifling a yawn. It was not the company, he assured himself. It had been a long ride from Lizard Gulch, and he was exhausted.

He was about to suggest they call it a night when Roberta chuckled naughtily and said, "There's something I've always wanted to try, Longarm. And I think you're just the man who would understand."

Longarm was dismayed. He had gone as limp as a warm noodle. "Oh? What's that?"

She was too shy to say it out loud. She lifted her head and whispered into his ear.

"Sounds great," he replied, chuckling. "I've always wanted to try that myself. But right now I'm truly worn out."

"Next time, maybe?"

"Next time for sure."

"Mmm," she murmured, kissing him, her tongue

thrusting deep once more in a fierce, insistent effort to arouse him.

But there was no more steam left in his engine.

"Night, darling," she said, pulling away. "It was lovely."

In a moment she had donned her nightgown and vanished off the ridge. He took a deep breath. Yes, sir. Next time they'd try that for sure. But right now, what he needed was sleep.

He rolled over, pulled the tarp over him, and with his right hand grasping the handle of his Colt, he slept.

The Pima band led by Tall Coyote was on the far side of the butte, but it took almost a full day for Longarm to reach it. When he did, he found the village nestled in a canyon between a long wall of red rock and a stream that followed a deep channel the length of the rock. Pine, some willows, and scrub cottonwoods provided what little vegetation there was between the stream and the Pima lodges. In the rock wall overlooking the village, caves had been fortified with rock and adobe to make ideal defensive ramparts.

As Longarm's mount splashed across the river, Tall Coyote rode out to greet him. There were few braves at his back, and as Longarm glanced into the village, he saw only a few women and children. The village looked almost deserted.

"I greet you with sad heart," said Tall Coyote.

Longarm pulled up. "Why is that, Tall Coyote?"

"Bird That Walks has taken my people. He is sure you are dead, and so now he takes the woman of the white diggers and makes a new home for himself and those braves who go with him."

60

"A new home?"

"Yes! Below the border, in the land of the Mexicans. There, he say, there will be no more white men or soldiers to follow him. If the Apache can live free there, so too can the Pima. Hear me, Longarm. I speak the truth."

"It is a sad day for Tall Coyote. I am sorry."

"A few stay with me. But only a few. Our band is broken."

"When did Bird That Walks leave?"

"Two days ago."

"I must go back to the dig. I do not want him to take the woman."

"She is your woman?"

Longarm hesitated for only a moment. "Yes."

"Tall Coyote will go with you. He has no home now. It would be a good way to die—helping his friend Longarm."

"I am honored."

Longarm had to wait for the old chief to get his battle dress and the rest of his paraphernalia, but at length he left his grieving village and set out with Longarm.

They traveled through the night and arrived by midmorning of the next day. The camp was in a turmoil. Bird That Walks and his renegades had attacked at sunset the day before and taken Roberta. The young chief had not killed any of the men, but two were left wounded: Nathan and Roberta's brother, James.

When the survivors of the attack saw Longarm ride in with the chief, they were furious. Longarm could not blame them. After all, Tall Coyote was the Pima chief whose word had been given solemnly that they could excavate at this site without retaliation from the band. The chief understood how matters now stood and said nothing as he remained on his horse and let Longarm interview the survivors. He went first to Pettigrew, who at once charged Longarm with being in cahoots with the Indians. Joining in, Wynne sneered at Longarm. He knew all about Roberta and Longarm—as did the entire camp—and he told Longarm that he was glad Roberta had been taken by the savages. She was no better than a whore.

Longarm flattened him with a single punch.

Gladstone and his two men were too shaken for calm conversation, so that left only Nathan. He was in the only surviving tent, propped on a cot alongside Roberta's brother, James. Both had been wounded by arrows which they had since pulled out, not very expertly. James was unconscious and it was obvious that Nathan was in considerable pain and had lost a great deal of blood. Despite all this, Nathan was the most coherent of them all.

"They circled us," he told Longarm, "yelling their fool heads off. It made my blood go cold, I tell you. Then they charged. We didn't know which way to shoot. And then they were on us and we didn't have any more weapons. They just snatched them away from us. I wish you had been here, Longarm."

"I do too. Go on."

"The leader was tall and had curious bird symbols on his shield. His nose was like a hawk's."

"He's called Bird That Walks."

"That so? You know him?"

"I heard about him. Go on."

"Well, as soon as we were disarmed, the Indians drew their bows and aimed at us. We thought we were

62

all goners. Then their leader dismounted, pulled a horse from his remuda, and approached Roberta. He motioned for her to get onto the horse. She screamed and pulled away. That was when James and I tried to stop the son of a bitch. But he just said something to his band, and before we knew it, we were pincushions. Luckily we took the shafts in the arms and thighs."

"Go on."

"By that time we all knew it was hopeless to fight. The chief caught Roberta up in his arms and flung her onto the pony."

"Didn't she struggle or try to jump off?"

"You bet she did. And she put up a pretty good fight, until they socked her on the jaw. Then one of the Indians tied a rope to her ankle, fed it under the pony's belly, and tied her other ankle. She couldn't fall off then, but she couldn't get off, either."

"How do you feel?"

"Not so good. I lost a lot of blood."

"I suggest you send for the doctor at Lizard Gulch. He's good enough. He took care of me and Charity."

"I'll do that."

"Now this is important, Nathan. Did you overhear the Indians say anything about destination?"

"I can't be sure. I told you, I don't know their lingo. But over and over as they started to ride out they called something that sounded like mut-tah-no-me."

"Thanks."

Longarm walked over to Tall Coyote. "What does this mean, mut-tah-no-me?"

"Ah! You mean Mah-tan-ohme!"

"Okay, Chief. That's a better pronunciation. What does it mean?"

"Two Peaks."

"You know where that is?"

"It is where the Apache hide in Mexico. Sometimes Geronimo go there when he is beat."

Longarm called Pettigrew over and nudged him into his son's tent. "Send Wynne into Lizard Gulch for the doctor. Both these men need a doctor's care."

"Are you sure they are wounded that seriously?"

"No, I am not, Pettigrew. You've got an alternative, though."

"And what might that be?"

"Wait and see if your son Nathan dies."

A week after they crossed the Mexican border, Tall Coyote pointed. Two Mexicans were driving some sheep up a slope. They were in white cotton pants and shirts and wore large, sugar-loaf sombreros to keep off the heat.

"I think I need big hat to keep off sun. Maybe blanket with hole in it, too."

Longarm nodded and turned his horse in the direction of the two sheepherders. He had long since stashed his badge away and done what he could to forget how far he had strayed from his original assignment, which was to protect the scientists from the Pima Indians. It was no use worrying about that now, he realized. He was operating in a land where law did not exist, and if he wanted to see Roberta again, he had no choice but to keep on going and worry about the legalities later.

When the Mexicans saw the two riders, one of them very obviously an Indian, they began to run.

"Ho! They give us sport!" Tall Coyote cried, using his quirt to speed his pony after them.

In a few moments the terrified Mexicans were overtaken and Tall Coyote circled the two sheepherders, Longarm riding at his side.

"What're you up to, Tall Coyote? I thought you meant to trade for a hat."

"Yes, I trade."

Dismounting, the old chief walked up to the two cowering Mexicans. He pointed to the hat on the taller one. The Mexican gave it to the Indian immediately. Then the chief pointed to the serape the other one was wearing. This was immediately handed over to Tall Coyote. Pleased, the chief put both items on and smiled up at Longarm.

"You see? I am protected from the heat and no one will know I am Pima Indian."

"Don't count on it, Chief."

Tall Coyote started for his pony.

"What're you going to give these two for the hat and serape?"

"I trade them like you say. I give them their life for blanket and tall hat. I think is good trade—if hat not leak."

Longarm flung a couple of silver dollars at the Mexicans, turned his horse, and rode off, a pleased Tall Coyote following after him.

"Apaches!" Tall Coyote said, pointing.

They were Apaches, all right, moving in a tight body, their captives herded in front of them, a smoking village at their rear. They looked as if they had just finished the raid and were now hurrying for the canyon entrance where Longarm and Tall Coyote were crouching.

He and Tall Coyote had been on a ledge high above

the canyon entrance when the chief caught sight of the dust cloud in the distance. It took about ten minutes for Longarm to catch sight of the dust cloud. They immediately descended to the canyon entrance, where they now waited, hidden in among a cluster of boulders.

Though it was close to dusk, there was enough light for Longarm to see the oncoming Apaches clearly. He counted close to a dozen Apaches pushing six or seven captives ahead of them, along with about five head of cattle and a lone goat. Only two of the Apaches were mounted, and these acted as a rear guard. As the Apaches got closer, Longarm saw that four of the captives were young children under ten years of age and that the older captives were Mexican women—and one old man trying desperately to keep up. Why the Apaches hadn't killed him was a puzzle to Longarm until he saw that the old man was carrying a toddler. The Apaches needed children, even children this young, and were sparing the old man in order to gain the baby.

"Could this be Geronimo?"

"Geronimo still in San Carlos. But he come here soon, I think. These Apaches are Chiricahua, his people. They wait for Geronimo to lead them."

"What do you want to do?"

"Kill Apaches."

"Those coming at us?"

"They are only Apaches I see."

"I don't like the odds," Longarm said.

"Then hide. I will not tell the Apaches you are here."

"I did not say I would not join you," Longarm said in some exasperation. "I said I didn't like the odds."

"Maybe you right. The odds are bad. We big fools if we attack now. We will follow Apache to their camp.

When they sleep we will slit their throats."

Longarm didn't know if he liked that idea any better than a surprise frontal assault. But as Tall Coyote slipped away into the rocks, Longarm followed without further argument.

The Apaches had found a large cave high in the Sierra Madres, one with a fine, level area just in front of it. On this level clearing they built their fires and their women did most of the camp's work. The captives were tied together with rawhide and dragged unceremoniously into the cave out of the way.

Longarm and the chief were perched on a ledge above the cave. They watched as one of the fires was built up and a victory dance took place around it. The Apaches made as much noise as it was possible for this small number of Apaches to make, and they expended a great deal of energy in the process, but Longarm had the feeling their hearts were not in it. They had just done what Apaches were supposed to do. They had attacked a village and kidnapped children and two young women. Then they had danced around a victory fire and told stories of their exploits, after which they gorged themselves on the meat of a fresh-killed goat and washed it down with whiskey. Even so, they were a tired, uninspired band, and Longarm realized Tall Coyote was correct. They were waiting for Geronimo.

"We wait hour, maybe two," said the chief.

"We could just steal in there and free the captives."

"You do that. I kill Apaches."

"You talk big. How are you gonna do that?"

"I use my knife until I am discovered. Then I use my Colt." He patted the big gun he had tucked into his belt.

67

"After that I use my war hatchet. I kill many Apache."

"And they're liable to kill you right back."

"Maybe yes, but I did not come here to live. I came here to kill Apache."

"And to find Bird That Walks, don't forget."

He thought a moment. "Yes. That is true. What do you want me to do?"

"Let me help you kill Apaches."

"Now you talk and I listen."

"You come up from beneath the slope. I'll lower myself down from here onto the ledge in front of the cave. I'll go inside it and cut loose the captives. Then I'll start using my own knife. When the Apaches wake up to what's happening, there'll be two sixguns instead of one to cut them down."

The old chief nodded. "Good plan. Simple. I will give you time to reach cave. When you leave cave, I will climb onto ledge."

"And then we kill Apaches."

"Then we kill Apaches."

Longarm was near the end of the rope when he let go and landed on cat feet just in front of the cave entrance. He had made a sound, however, and he heard an Apache sleeping less than ten feet away stir. He froze and waited. After he began to hear regular breathing once again, Longarm entered the cool interior of the cave.

He crouched for a long while, waiting for his eyes to get accustomed to the darkness. At last he caught sight of the two women. He hurried to the side of the nearest one and placed his hand over her mouth. As she struggled to free herself, he leaned close to her ear.

"Por favor, please. Be silent. I come to help."

His tone of voice, if not his feeble Spanish, did the trick. The woman stopped struggling. He took his hand away from her mouth.

"Ees all right," she whispered. "I speak the English."

He swiftly cut through her rawhide bonds and let her wake the other woman so that Longarm could cut her free as well. Then Longarm sat back and let the two women arouse the children as quietly as possible. They made a few sleepy queries, but were quiet enough not to arouse the Apaches outside. The old man, the babe still in his arms, could not be awakened, however.

The women beckoned Longarm over. He felt the old man's jugular. It was no longer pulsing. The excitement and the strenuous climb to this ledge had been too much for him. Longarm glanced at the women and shook his head. One of them smothered a tiny cry, then leaned forward and kissed the old man's wrinkled forehead. The other woman took the babe up in her arms. Fortunately, it still slept soundly.

Longarm beckoned them farther back into the cave, then crept to its entrance and moved out of the cave, still on his hands and knees, heading for the nearest sleeping Apache. A mean, powerful chuckle came from behind him. At once Longarm knew it was the Apache he had awakened earlier. Without conscious thought, Longarm whirled, thrusting his knife up. He caught the Apache in the belly. Plunging the knife in as deep as he could get it, Longarm jumped up, his stiffened forearm lifting the Apache into the air. The Indian struggled like a bullfighter impaled on a horn, screaming all the while.

Longarm flung him at another Apache racing toward him, then unholstered his Colt and began blasting at the aroused forms leaping to their feet all around him. As he cut them down, Longarm saw the chief materializing on the ledge. In a second he was firing also—and in a surprisingly short time the ledge was littered with the sprawled, bleeding bodies of dead and wounded Apaches.

"Ho!" cried Tall Coyote, stepping over a downed Apache, his dark face bright with triumph. "Tonight we kill many Apaches. Geronimo not find these when he come south next time."

"Look out!" cried one of the women standing in the cave entrance.

But her cry came too late. The Apache who had risen from the ledge plunged his lance deep into Tall Coyote's back. As the old chief collapsed face down onto the ledge, Longarm pulled out his derringer, strode toward the Apache, and sent two .44 cartridges into his head.

After the Apache struck the ground, Longarm kicked him to make sure he was dead. Then he reloaded his Colt and passed among the sprawled Apaches, finishing off any that were still alive. Only then did he kneel beside Tall Coyote to see what—if anything—he could do for him.

There wasn't much.

The blade had been thrust deep into the old chief's back. As carefully as possible, Longarm removed the lance and rolled the old chief over. Tall Coyote opened his eyes.

"Longarm. Get Bird That Walks for me. And tell my band how many Apache I kill this night."

"It is many. I will tell them."

"Good. Maybe then the foolish braves will return to their home."

"I hope so. But you should rest now. That's a bad wound."

"No. It is not bad wound. It is my last wound." He smiled grimly. "This chief is old fool. He crow so loud, he wake dead Apache. So dead Apache kill him. I die now. Goodbye."

Tall Coyote closed his eyes and died.

Chapter 4

In the morning, with Longarm escorting them, the captives started back to their village, arriving early in the afternoon. At sight of the returning captives, the villagers' cries of welcome filled the air. This was nothing less than a miracle. Few, if any, Mexicans carried off by the Apaches ever returned to their villages—and this had been true for close to a century. These Mexican villagers stood alone against the successive waves of Apaches and Comanches who rode into their land to kill, plunder, and rape at will, and then carried off as slaves those children and young women they deemed useful.

The old man, whose name was Alejandro, had no family, but the woman whose baby he had saved from an Apache's fury covered the old man's slack face with kisses. Then she, her husband, and their relatives promptly made ready for his funeral. Longarm was asked to stay for the sad but proud occasion. The old man had been loved by all who knew him, and now he was to be buried as a hero.

The village boasted a modest cantina and in a small room at its rear, Longarm had been put up and fed, with the cantina's owner not even considering the possibility that he should pay. Indeed, Longarm was now regarded by the villagers as some kind of powerful presence, a *norteamericano* whose miraculous appearance had magically restored two women to their husbands, and the stolen babe and captured children to their families.

If the old man was a hero, Longarm was looked upon almost as a god. That he was not a Mexican made no difference to these simple villagers. For them, he could do no wrong.

Longarm had a visitor his first night. She did not bother to knock. He saw the door open and watched a slim figure slip inside his room. Closing the door firmly behind her, she padded on bare feet over to his bed.

"I am here," she said in excellent English, "to comfort the great gringo hero." There was a mischievous note in her voice that Longarm did not mind at all, especially when he felt her slim, warm body moving under the covers next to him.

He was going to ask her who in hell she was, speaking in such good English, when he felt her hand reaching down to check his temperature. It was steaming and, figuring he could find out who she was later, he just rolled atop her, wedged her naked thighs open with his knees, and plunged into her with no further conversation.

Whoever she was, she sure seemed to enjoy it very much indeed. He enjoyed it, too. It was a welcome relief from the memory of the dead Apaches littering that ledge in front of the cave entrance, and the death of a fine Pima chieftain.

Abruptly, she stretched her legs out to both sides and gasped, "I'm *coming!*"

He was right on schedule himself and came in her at the same time. They went weakly limp in each other's arms and she said, "That was wonderful. Do you suppose we could do it some more?"

"The night is young."

"You're so understanding!" She laughed softly, flinging her arms around his neck and squeezing him delightedly. "Can we start now?"

"In a minute. I didn't hold back at all, so I need time to catch my second wind. Despite all the evidence to the contrary, I'm only human."

"Nonsense!"

"Who are you?"

"Jenny Johnston."

"Where are you from?"

"Texas."

"What in hell are you doing down here?"

"When I was a small girl I decided I would travel and see the world. I sure as hell knew that Texas wasn't it. So when a smart-talking, high-steppin' Mexican who played a mean guitar happened by, singing about his hacienda south of the border, I went right along with him."

"Smart move."

"I'll say. I woke up in a room filled with cockroaches and scorpions somewhere in Chihuahua—alone."

"He didn't even leave the guitar."

"No. But he left a large bill at the local cantina and the rooming house. When I finished paying them both off, I found myself taken in hand by a gentle old man, who brought me here."

"Alejandro?"

"Yes."

"He took you in."

"I can honestly say I made his last days happy. Toward the end he made very few demands on me, and I almost regarded him as my father. It was strange."

"So now you come to me."

"I must admit, it is nice to be with a fully equipped man once more. And I am sure Alejandro understands."

Longarm nodded, took out a cheroot, and lit up.

"What about me?"

He laughed, handed her one, and lit it for her. For a long while they smoked without saying a word. The moonlight filtering in through the window gave him a pretty good look at her. She was a lush, wide-hipped young lady, with a profusion of dark curls and eyes that glowed at him in the dim light.

"What were you and that Indian doing down here, gringo?" she asked.

"Looking for a kidnapped woman."

"Who took her? Apaches?"

"No, a Pima chief and some young hotheads with him. The chief has decided to make Mexico his new home. Trying to act like Apaches, from the sound of it."

"The Pima hate the Apache. And the Apache truly fear the Pima. The only ones who can track the Apache are the Pima. It is a great enmity, over many, many years."

"That doesn't help me find the Pimas and the woman they've taken."

"This woman. Is she yours?"

"No, but I know her well."

76

"As well as you know me?"

"Yes."

"I see."

He caught something in her voice. "Have you seen these Pimas or heard anything about the woman with them?"

"I have heard nothing. For the past weeks we were fearing a raid by the Apaches. We knew they were nearby. And then they came."

She shuddered and leaned her head against his shoulder. As she did so, Longarm discovered he was ready again. Finishing his smoke, he stubbed it out, then pulled her close. She got rid of her smoke just as quickly. They coupled quickly, eagerly, and in a few minutes shared another orgasm.

"Now let me get on top," she said, blowing a thick lock of dark hair aside. "The old man, he loved this, and I can make it last very long."

"You sure? I'm really down."

"Trust me. I have had much experience."

He leaned back and let her have her way with him.

The next day, Longarm and Jenny attended Alejandro's funeral together. Then the mayor announced a festival in Longarm's honor. It was to be held two days later. That night, Longarm slipped out of the village—intending to leave as mysteriously as he had arrived, a suitable finale to this wondrous tale.

He was a few miles north of the village, heading back toward the peaks of the Sierra Madre looming into the night sky, when he heard hoofbeats closing on him from behind. He pulled up and turned in his saddle. It was Jenny.

"Go back," he told her when she reached him.

"You need help."

"Not that kind. I've got to find those Pimas."

"I know. That's why I'm joining you. I know where they are."

"You said you knew nothing."

"I lied."

"Why?"

"I was jealous of this woman."

"All right, then. Help me."

"We go south, toward Caborca. The white woman you are seeking is no longer with the Pima Indians. She was taken from them by the *rurales* based in Caborca. They are a mean bunch."

"What happened to the Pimas?"

"Their leader got away with about half his men. Many have reported seeing them heading north, back to Arizona."

"How do you know all this?"

"Word travels faster than the wind between our villages. It is our only protection. When the Apaches attacked we were ready. Had we not been waiting, the Apaches would have done us much more harm."

"You've told me. Now go on back to your village."

"It is not my village. And the old man is dead. Now I am free to go where I want."

"Then go back to Texas. You're a Texan, not a Mexican."

"I wonder. Maybe I am really a Mexican in my heart."

"Then you won't go back to the village?"

"No."

"Where will you go?"

She smiled brilliantly. "With you."

What was it, Longarm wondered, that made these wild young ladies so eager to ride with him? He shrugged. "Okay," he told Jenny. "We ride together as far as Caborca."

Two days later they rode into Caborca. It was a pretty fair-sized town. Most of the squat adobe buildings faced onto a large plaza. The largest building was the church across from the cantina. The rest of the buildings were little more than mud huts with doorways so low that the people had to duck their heads to enter. Grass grew on the flat roofs, and the walls surrounding the houses were fitted with firing ports. Aside from the church, the most impressive building was a long, sprawling, single-story building, its portico held up by rough-hewn tree trunks. The rafter beams sticking out from under the roofline looked like cannon barrels. The main door was recessed and made of heavy planks several feet wide and many inches thick. This, Longarm had no doubt, was the Palacio Federal, the headquarters of the local *rurales*.

They found a hotel at the corner of the plaza, an adobe two-story affair. As they dismounted in front of it, they saw three or four *rurales* emerging from the long building, watching them with bright eyes. Occasional explosions of laughter erupted from their midst, the cruel, barking sound filling the quiet square. The townspeople seemed to have vanished into the cool shadows of their dwellings, perhaps to watch.

Longarm escorted Jenny into the hotel. Behind the front desk a very nervous clerk awaited them.

"Pardon, *señor*," he said to Longarm. "Forgive me, but I must ask this one thing. Have you register with the *rurales?*"

79

"Not yet."

"I suggest you do so, *señor*."

"Now?"

The desk clerk swallowed unhappily. *"Sí."*

"Wait here," he told Jenny, and strode from the hotel.

More members of the *rurales* had gathered, and only reluctantly did they part before the tall *norteamericano* who had just ridden so boldly into their town with his woman. As Longarm pushed through them, they grinned at him and nudged each other. They were like vultures on a branch, measuring portions they would soon be tearing from a carcass.

Inside, Longarm found himself in a long, cool corridor. At its end he spied an open door, a dim, flickering light coming from within the room it led into. He moved down the corridor and entered the room. A pistol-belted *rurale* was leaning back in a wooden chair just inside the door, his high-crowned sombrero pulled down over his eyes to shield them from the glare of the smoking oil lamp on the battered desk beside him.

Longarm cleared his throat.

The Mexican pushed his hat up and stared at him.

"Que quieres, hombre?" he growled.

"The clerk across the street told me I had to register," Longarm told him, unwilling to attempt any Spanish. It had been a long ride and he was just not up to it. "Show me the book and I'll sign it."

"Registrar?" the *rurale* asked.

Longarm nodded.

"Norteamericano?"

Again Longarm nodded.

Reluctantly, the *rurale* pushed his chair forward onto all four of its legs, then stood up and disappeared through a door in the back of the room.

A moment later the *rurale* returned, followed almost at once by a clean-shaven officer who had on both the gold-embroidered *charro* jacket and the braid-lined trousers that officers of the *rurales* wore. He stopped in the doorway and gazed with alert brown eyes at Longarm.

"Norteamericano a registrar?" he asked.

"That's right. The desk clerk at the hotel sent me over."

The officer smiled. "A wise precaution, I assure you."

Graciously, the officer escorted Longarm into his office and closed the door behind him. Extending his hand, he shook Longarm's and introduced himself.

"I am Captain Bartolome Molina."

"Custis Long, deputy U.S. marshal out of Denver."

Molina's eyebrows lifted. "Denver? You are a long way from Denver, *señor.*"

"Don't I know it."

"What is it you seek in this quiet village?"

"A Miss Roberta Prescott. A band of Pima Indians kidnapped her and crossed the border into Mexico. The last I heard, the *rurales* had taught them a lesson and taken the woman from them."

"To be safe, I am sure."

"Of course."

Captain Molina smiled brilliantly. "This woman you speak of, she is already here in this town. She was not in such good condition when we take her from the Pimas. Now she is much better. She stays with *el Patron* at his hacienda outside of town."

"This feller got a name?"

"Esteban Sanchez."

"Much obliged, Captain." Longarm walked over to the registry on the table, took the pen out of the inkwell, and signed his name on the first vacant line. Then he placed the pen back into the inkwell and headed for the door.

"I would be glad to escort you to *el Patron's* hacienda," the captain told Longarm.

"That's decent of you. But I guess I can find it all right."

"No, *señor,*" the captain said, his voice gaining a sudden edge, his eyes coldly alert.

"You do not want me to go alone? Is this Sanchez dangerous?"

"We do not think he is loyal to Diaz. He is dangerous man. So I think it would be best if my men and I, we escort you."

Longarm shrugged. "What about first thing in the morning?"

"Excellent."

Once he was alone with Jenny in their hotel room, Longarm walked over to the window and looked across the street at the Palacio Federal. The crew of *rurales* was gone now. In its place were two sullen *rurales,* their chests crossed with cartridge belts, rifles at their sides. And they were staring fixedly at the hotel.

"I got the feeling we just landed in the midst of something hot," Longarm told Jenny as he left the window. "You got any idea what it might be?"

"Sure."

"What?"

"Elections."

Longarm frowned. "You want to explain that?"

"In Mexico, elections are very noisy. Very deadly. They are really small revolutions."

"I thought Diaz was in control."

"He is in control now. But maybe not tomorrow. He has just announced he will not run for president again. Now every little general and every little group of *rurales* are looking to see which way to jump. The big landowners who backed Diaz are looking for someone to take his place, and so are those who have been waiting for this chance to take over the government."

Longarm glanced out the window at the Palacio Federal. Perhaps Captain Molina was looking for a place to jump, also, which might explain why he was so anxious for a pretext to ride out to Esteban Sanchez's hacienda.

"Let's get some rest," Longarm told her, "then go downstairs to eat. But don't relax any. We're going to be slipping out of this town as soon as it's dark enough for us to make it without being caught."

"Where are we going?"

"To a hacienda outside of town. Roberta is there, but as usual nothing is as simple as it might be."

A moment later, as Jenny began to peel off his pants, he said hopelessly, "I meant it, Jenny. We need to get some rest."

"Maybe you do," she told him happily. "But I think maybe you will rest better afterward."

She sat back and slipped her blouse off her shoulders. Longarm sighed and reached up for her. Maybe he *would* sleep better afterwards, at that.

The livery where they had left their horses was behind the hotel, effectively blocking its entrance from the Palacio Federal. Ducking their heads, they rode out into the night and headed out of town, keeping to the back alleys. The clerk had given good directions to *el Patron's* hacienda and Longarm had given him what he hoped would be enough gold coins to keep the young man's mouth shut.

The moon was high, clear in a black sky alight with stars. They traveled southwest along a deeply rutted road and soon came in sight of a high gate, the head and horns of a steer nailed to the crossbeam. They passed under it and continued on for some distance before they saw, ahead of them on a slight crown, the dark outline of a magnificent mansion and the wall that surrounded it. As they rode closer, two armed *pistoleros* stepped out of the shadows and lifted their rifles. Longarm and Jenny pulled up quickly.

The men's pistol belts were sagging under the weight of a pair of holstered pistols. But that was not enough. Long knives and ancient flintlocks were stuck in their belts also. Without a word, the *pistoleros* motioned with their rifles for Longarm and Jenny to dismount.

"I have come to see *el Patron*," Longarm told the two, as he dismounted.

As Jenny jumped down beside him, a tall gentleman strode out of the darkness toward them. It was obvious he was the *Patron*.

A tall man, an inch shorter than Longarm, he was exceedingly lanky. His complexion was olive, his hair, which he combed straight back from his wide forehead, was jet-black. His nose was high-bridged and thin, his eyes brown. He had long sideburns in addition to a well-oiled mustache. His lips were full, his mouth wide and expressive. He wore a suit of dark purple velvet, cut *charro*-style, a short jacket over a silken shirt, and tight-fitting trousers that flared at mid-calf over gleaming, highly polished boots.

"I am *el Patron*," he said. "And who are you—and why would you be riding onto my grounds at this hour?"

Longarm introduced Jenny and himself to Esteban Sanchez, then said, "I have come for Roberta Prescott. It is said she is here with you."

"Ah! Then you must be the famous Longarm!"

"How do you know that?"

"Roberta talk of you much. I must admit, at times I am jealous. She say you will come for her. And now I see she is right."

"How is she?"

"Better—and getting better." Sanchez looked at Jenny. "And who is your companion. Is she also a deputy U. S. marshal?"

"She knows the country. And it was she who told me where to find Roberta."

Sanchez nodded. "Yes, everyone hears of this beautiful captive of the Indians and of her rescue by the *rurales*. It is not a pleasant story, and talk of this thing fills many evenings. Come, she is asleep now, but I do not think she will mind if I wake her!"

One look at Longarm and Roberta jumped out of her bed and flung herself into his arms. Longarm was astounded and touched. This was a far cry from the imperious, independent woman he had known at the dig.

"Oh, Longarm!" she cried. "I knew you'd come for me!"

Sanchez glanced nervously at Jenny and then at Roberta, a perplexed frown on his face. "Was it so bad here with me, Roberta?"

"Oh, no, Esteban! I do not mean that," she cried. "You have been so kind! But Longarm has come so far for me—as I knew he would!"

"How do you feel, Roberta?" Longarm asked.

"It was horrible! Whatever you do, you must kill that Indian!"

"Bird That Walks?"

"He is Animal That Stinks!" Roberta stiffened in his arms. "And the *rurales!* They were no better than the savages. They were worse! They laughed and drank while they passed me around like—!"

To remember it again was too much for her. She shuddered, then began to sob uncontrollably. A slim, grim-faced *mestiza* woman hurried into the bedroom and pulled Roberta gently from Longarm's arms, then helped her back into her bed. Burying her face in her pillow, Roberta continued to sob, no longer interested, it seemed, in talking to Longarm or anyone else. She sobbed with the intensity of a child whose favorite doll has been lost forever.

Longarm held up long enough to tuck the covers up around Roberta's neck and kiss her lightly on the cheek. Then he left the room with Sanchez and Jenny. Sanchez escorted them out to a table on the patio. He had wine brought, and while a cool breeze sighed through the leafy trellis overhanging the patio, Longarm and Jenny listened while Sanchez told them what he did when he heard of the *norteamericano* woman the *rurales* had liberated from the Indians.

"Up until then," Sanchez explained, "I remain aloof from local politics. I do not interfere. Here on my hacienda I am king. I have my *pistoleros* who will fight to the last drop of blood for this land and for my family. So no one bothers me. The *rurales* can have the rest of the world, for all I care."

He paused for a moment to stare balefully out into the darkness.

"But some things," he said, resuming at last, "one cannot allow. It is too terrible."

"So you rode into town and took her from the *rurales*."

"Yes. We surrounded the Palacio Federal and demanded her release."

"Molina didn't put up any argument?"

"He said he would make us pay. He said no filthy landowner could tell the *rurales* what to do. He said many other things. I did not listen to him. Now, I wait. If Diaz does not run for president again, I think there will be much trouble in this country."

"As soon as Roberta is ready to leave, we will take her back," Longarm said.

"No," said Jenny.

Longarm turned to look at her.

"I think maybe I shall stay here with *Señor* Sanchez."

Sanchez smiled. "That would be my pleasure, *señorita*."

"Molina had planned on taking us out here first thing in the morning, *Señor* Sanchez," Longarm told the man, leaning back in his chair to study *el Patron's* reaction.

"He was going to use you then as an excuse to get into these gates. That is interesting," the wealthy man observed. "You think he's about ready to make his move, do you?"

"Yes, I do," said Longarm.

"Thank you, my friend, for warning me," Sanchez said.

"What are you going to do?"

"Alert my men. We will be ready when he comes!"

"He has no excuse now. Jenny and I have left the hotel," said Longarm.

"So what do you suggest?"

"It is only a little before midnight. The whole night is before us. We are less than a mile from town. Call your men together. I say you should make your own move, before the captain does."

"Tonight?"

"Yes."

"But what will we do when we capture the *rurales?* How will we explain it to the government?" Sanchez looked worried.

Jenny spoke up then, quickly and forcefully. *"El Patron,* is there anyone in the Diaz government you can trust?"

"Only one."

"Who is he?"

"General Ramos."

"Send someone to him. Tell him you are retaking the town, that the *rurales* here have revolted."

"But they have done no such thing!"

Jenny shrugged. "Are you so sure? I thought I heard such talk while I was walking the streets. There is much sentiment for a revolution. With Diaz leaving, a revolution is inevitable. Did you not hear such whispers, Longarm?"

He took the bait quickly. "Yes, I did."

"You see, *señor,* you must send to this general and

you must act. At once. You will be a hero of the republic. Perhaps Diaz will see the danger of letting go. Perhaps he will run again."

Sanchez looked at Longarm. "We will take the *rurales'* garrison tonight—and *then* we will send word to General Ramos."

Longarm got to his feet. "Let's go, then."

The *pistoleros* were approaching from the back and the time Sanchez had given them to surround the place was now up. The two *rurales* on guard at the front door of the Palacio Federal were slumped wearily back against the wall on either side of the door. One was smoking a cigarette; the other appeared to be dozing, his rifle propping him up. Occasionally, the two men stirred themselves enough to speak softly to each other—a complaint, usually, at this miserable guard duty.

Moving closer to them through the darkness, Longarm and Esteban could hear them more and more clearly. Esteban held up suddenly and turned to Longarm.

"I just heard the unhappy words of the one smoking," he whispered.

"What'd he say?"

Esteban smiled coldly. "They would be too tired to march out tomorrow morning to my hacienda. So you see? It is true, what you thought. Captain Molina was coming for me tomorrow."

Esteban turned then and crept closer to the two guards. When they were within fifty yards, Esteban said, "You take the nearest one. I'll take the one smoking."

Longarm nodded. Both men had impressed on the *pistoleros* that there was to be as little bloodshed as possible. The victory over this hated garrison of *rurales* would be all the greater if they could take them without a shot and with no loss of life. For this reason, though Longarm approached the dozing guard with his Colt drawn, he planned to club the guard, not shoot him.

Esteban slipped into the shadows to come at his guard from the other side. Longarm waited. When he glimpsed Esteban moving closer to the rurale on the other side of the entrance, Longarm darted to the side of the building and, keeping himself in its shadows, slipped closer to his man. Flattened against the wall within ten feet of him, Longarm waited. When he saw Esteban make his rush, Longarm stepped away from the building and snatched away the *rurale's* rifle. He came awake suddenly, a confused look on his face.

"Sorry," Longarm muttered, as he brought the barrel of his Colt down onto the *rurale's* head.

The man crumpled to the ground and went back to sleep.

Esteban had despatched his man just as neatly. Longarm pulled open the door and stepped inside, Esteban right behind him. Esteban closed the door softly and the two stood for a minute in the cool darkness, getting their bearings. The only sound was the snoring coming from further down the long corridor.

They moved down the corridor. On their left a double door was ajar and the snoring of many men came from beyond it. Longarm nudged the door open. About ten cots were visible in the dim light, five against each wall. On each cot slumped a *rurale,* some fully dressed with only their boots off, others sprawled naked—and all of them sleeping with the enthusiasm of men who have drunk their fill.

Esteban's *pistoleros* appeared at the end of the corridor. Esteban beckoned them closer. There were a dozen men in all, but they moved as soundlessly as shadows and in a moment were crowding around Longarm and Esteban, peering into the room where the *rurales* were sleeping.

"There's another roomful farther down," Esteban's lieutenant, Jose, muttered.

"Divide your men and take both rooms," Esteban told him. "Longarm and I will see to Captain Molina."

"I do not know where he sleeps," said Jose.

"Neither do we. But he is in here somewhere. We will find him."

Longarm and Esteban moved off down the corridor, leaving the *rurales* to Jose. They tried the captain's office, but it was empty. There were stairs leading to the second floor at the end of the corridor. As they started up them, sounds of scuffling and sleepy cries of alarm drifted up past them as the *pistoleros* made their move. Longarm and Esteban had reached the second floor and were moving down it swiftly to a door ahead of them when a shot rang out from below, and then another shot.

A lantern came on in the room they were heading toward. Longarm heard Captain Molina's sudden curse —and then the startled cry of a woman. By that time he had reached the door. He kicked it open.

Molina was still in bed, a big Colt in his hand, his arm around a naked woman he was using as a shield. She was big-busted, with a dark whorl of hair framing her white, terrified face. Esteban pushed Longarm to one side just as the Colt in Molina's hand bucked. Este-

91

ban was driven against the door jamb by the force of the slug. As Molina shifted his muzzle to Longarm, Longarm dove onto the bed and swiped the big gun out of Molina's hand. It went clattering heavily to the floor, discharging when it struck the wall.

By that time Longarm was standing up on the bed, tearing the girl from Molina's arms. As the girl struck the floor beside the bed, Longarm hauled Molina upright and rapped him smartly across the face with his own Colt. The captain's nose splattered, sending blood flying, and he collapsed unconscious to the floor.

"Behind you!" the girl screamed.

Longarm flung himself around as two *rurales* appeared in the open doorway, guns drawn. Before they could fire, Esteban cut them down from where he was sitting on the floor.

He grinned feebly at Longarm. Longarm jumped off the bed to examine *el Patron*. The bullet had caught him in the chest on the left side. Longarm pulled Esteban closer and peered at his back. The exit wound was ugly, but at least Esteban was no longer carrying the slug.

Jose rushed into the room. One look at his wounded leader and he went quickly down on one knee beside him. He inquired if Esteban was all right. Esteban waved off the question and asked for an accounting of the battle below.

Jose stood up and smiled proudly down at Esteban. "We have kill two *rurales*, and wound three more. That is all. The rest are very quiet now. They wonder. Are we going to hang them?"

"Throw them all in their own jail," Esteban said, with some satisfaction. "Tell them we will feed them well if they make no more trouble for us."

Jose nodded and hurried from the room.

The naked girl was crouching in a corner of the room, obviously terrified.

"What is your name?" Esteban asked her in Spanish.

She answered quickly, fearfully. "Delores Topiana."

"You are this dog's woman?"

"I hate him!" she said, spitting in his direction. "He is filth!"

"Get out!"

She snatched up her clothes lying across a chair and fled the room. Painfully, Esteban pulled himself to his feet and walked over to where Captain Molina lay crumpled on the floor, his shattered nose releasing a steady rivulet of blood over his face and onto the floor.

"He is very vain, that one," commented Esteban. "He will be very unhappy with what you have done to his nose."

"What'll we do with him?"

"I have a stockade in back of my house. I will keep him there until the general arrives."

"Then we're finished here."

"Yes—and so am I. Help me to my horse, Longarm."

Longarm did not have to be asked. He had come to like Esteban Sanchez. A few minutes before, his quick thinking might just have saved Longarm's life.

General Ramos arrived two days later with excellent news. Diaz had heard the rumbling in his land, had seen the signs of dislocation everywhere as his house of cards seemed about to collapse. It was not difficult for those who supported him to convince him to run for president again.

A week later, there was a new, positively loyal contingent of *rurales* in the Palacio Federal. Captain Molina was ready for his trip to Mexico City with the general to explain his unique manner of keeping peace in Caborca, and Longarm decided it was time to get in touch with Billy Vail.

He was on the patio with a pale but alert Esteban, along with Jenny, who had become Esteban's companion and nurse, and General Ramos. It was late in the evening, and the general had just remarked that the messenger who had arrived a few hours before had brought news that the countryside was quieting down and that not a single telegraph line was down.

"Good," said Longarm. "There is no telegraph office in Caborca. But I understand there is one a few miles south in Deldora."

"Yes, there is."

"Will you pass through it on your way to Mexico City?"

"I will."

"Then I would appreciate it, General, if you would send a telegram to Denver for me. As I have explained to Esteban, Marshal Vail must be wondering what in hell I am doing down here in Mexico."

The general laughed. "Write out your message, Longarm. I will be glad to send it."

Jenny spoke up. "What will you tell him, Longarm?"

"That I've found one member of the expedition I was supposed to look after—and that I will be bringing her back soon."

"You are sure of that, are you?" Esteban asked, frowning.

"Roberta's going to have to come out of her funk," Longarm told him. "I think we've babied her enough already."

"Babied her? Are you serious?"

"I am," Longarm replied.

"Well . . . I must admit I have run out of solutions. She seems all right for a while, and then she goes back into her sobbing. It is most disquieting."

Longarm looked at the general. "I'll have my message for you before you leave in the morning, General."

"Fine."

Longarm excused himself and went to Roberta's bedroom. He knocked softly, then pushed the door open. The lamp on her night table was still lit, but it was turned down quite low. The chimney was nearly black. The windows were open, but the room was stuffy, despite the night breeze coming in off the desert.

Roberta did not turn to face him when he entered. He had already told her that her brother had more than likely survived the Pima attack on the dig and that Nathan was alive as well. Until he told her of this, she had mistakenly concluded that both Nathan and her brother had been killed in the attack.

He sat down on the side of the bed. Roberta turned to face him. She looked terrible. Her cheeks were hollow, her eyes sunken into dark sockets, staring out at him as from a great distance. He took her hands in his and smiled.

She smiled wanly back, but her heart was not in it.

"They sure did a job on you," Longarm remarked sadly.

She pushed herself back up onto the pillow and brushed some strands of hair off her forehead. "Yes," she said, her voice low.

"I came a long way for you, but I guess I got here too late."

"Too late?"

"Yep."

"What do you mean?" There was a faint trace of alarm in her voice.

"Just what I said. There's no way you'll ever get over what those bastards did to you. You'll likely carry the scars inside you till the day you die. It'll make you feel squeamish, unfit. You'll never be the same. It wouldn't do me any good to take you back now."

"It wouldn't?" Alarm now showed in her eyes.

"Nope. I've seen this happen before. Women taken by the Indians. And then by the *rurales*. Used like you were. A woman ain't fit for decent use after such a thing. Best thing would be for you to stay here and let Esteban take care of you."

"He has other interests now," she said.

"Oh?"

"That Texan you brought with you. Jenny!"

"They do seem to get along, don't they." It was not a question.

"Yes," she snapped. "They do."

Longarm noticed that some color had returned to her cheeks and maybe a little fire had sprung into her eyes. But he did not change his resigned tone.

"So it's goodbye, Roberta. I'm pulling out first thing in the morning."

"I think you're wrong."

"Wrong? About what?"

"What you said...me being ruined for life. My being unfit for decent use after such a thing. I never gave in willingly. I fought every inch. I'm not ashamed."

"You sure seem pretty broken up to me."

"Do I?"

He nodded sadly.

Her hand flew to her face. She felt of her cheeks and her chin, then her arms, noting how thin they were. "I'm thin."

"Yep."

"And my hair's a mess."

He didn't bother to deny it.

"You're not taking me back with you?" she asked.

"It'll be a long ride—and you're in no condition for it, I figure. Mentally or physically."

"But you said James is probably alive—and Nathan."

"That's right."

"Then I have to go back!"

"Well, now, Roberta, I wouldn't be so sure of that if I were you."

"You aren't me! And it's not true what you said. I'm not ruined. And if you'd give me half a chance I'd *prove* it to you!"

"Right now?"

"Right now!"

He laughed and stood up. "Not right now, Roberta. Later, maybe. But I'm pulling out first thing in the morning. If you're willing to make the long ride back to Arizona with me, I'll be waiting for you at the stables."

"I'll be there," she said firmly.

This time, as Longarm looked at her, there was no doubt at all. Roberta Prescott had fire in her eyes. She was on the mend. She would be as good as new when she reached Arizona and the Sonora desert digs.

Chapter 5

The first thing Longarm did after he checked Roberta into the hotel in Lizard Gulch was to walk over to the telegraph office to see if Billy Vail had answered the telegram General Ramos had sent off for him. Vail had.

> WHAT IN BLAZES YOU DOING IN MEXICO
> STOP GET BACK TO US AT ONCE STOP
> STATE DEPARTMENT PREDICTS MEXICAN
> REVOLUTION STOP WHAT ABOUT SMITH-
> SONIAN PEOPLE STOP TELEGRAPH ME IM-
> MEDIATELY WHEN YOU GET BACK STOP
> WHAT IS GOING ON STOP VAIL

Longarm sent an answering telegram to Vail, admitting he was as much in the dark as Vail was. Then, grinning to himself, he left the telegraph office, washed off his tonsils at the saloon next to the hotel, then went upstairs to Roberta's room.

"Did Marshal Vail get your telegram?" Roberta asked.

She was standing in the darkening room, staring down at the broad main street, looking toward the water tower sitting beside the tracks halfway out of town.

"Yep." He handed her the telegram. She took it and, holding it up to the light still coming from the red sky, read it, then handed it back to Longarm.

"If he doesn't know why you went into Mexico, why do you have to tell him about me—or anyone else, for that matter?"

"Who said I was going to?"

"Thank you, Longarm. I knew I could count on you. But I still want you to get Bird That Walks for me."

"I don't know if I can promise you that, Roberta. We're back in the United States now, but we don't know if he and the remnants of his band ever got back here. Besides, the Pima have the reputation of never having harmed a U.S. citizen."

"I don't care about the Pima's damned reputation. You and I know better, Longarm. And so do my brother and the others. Bird That Walks and his band of savages ought to be burned alive."

As she spoke, she hugged herself and turned her back on him to look out the window. There was very little light left in the sky by this time, and behind Longarm the room was almost completely dark.

"If you want what happened to be forgotten, Roberta, maybe you'll have to put a cap on that anger."

She turned away from the window, then walked over to the bed and sat down on the edge of it. Folding her hands in her lap, she nodded wearily. "I suppose you are right, Longarm. Right now, all I want to do is see James again and get back to work. That's what I need."

"Maybe you're right," he said hopefully. "We'll be heading for the dig first thing tomorrow morning."

Before checking into the hotel, they had spoken to Doc Winslow. Both Nathan and Roberta's brother had survived their wounds, the doctor told them, without any complications, and were back out at the excavation site.

"Thanks, Longarm. I mean, for being so understanding and all. I must seem so silly to you."

"Of course not, Roberta. You mustn't think that."

Brushing an errant lock of hair out of her eyes, she smiled at him almost shyly. "You're a dear, Longarm. You'll see. I'll be ready at the crack of dawn."

Longarm started for the door. "Guess I'll go down for a nightcap."

"Are you going to sleep in here with me tonight?"

"I got a room down the hall, Roberta. Number fourteen."

"Oh." She looked quickly away from him toward the dark window.

He paused. He wanted to tell her it had nothing to do with her being used by the savages or by the *rurales,* but he couldn't get it out. He was as tongue-tied as she was, it seemed. All during the ride north, the wall between them had seemed to grow higher and more solid.

And all because of something neither dared mention.

"Night, Roberta."

"Good night, Longarm."

As Longarm found a corner table in the saloon and nursed his Maryland rye, he reflected on Roberta's condition and their dilemma. There had been many nights during the ride north into Arizona when he had found himself staring up at the stars, aware of her not less than ten feet away, and wanting her.

But Roberta was too frightened to let him near her. She dressed and undressed in the bushes and acted painfully shy whenever he passed close beside her. She was like a spooked pony, ready to rear at the first rustle of a branch or movement of a cloud across the sun.

He could tell that she still suffered a genuine feeling of unworthiness. In Caborca Longarm had told Esteban he was babying her, and Longarm had been able to jolt her out of her self-pity long enough at least to get her this far. Now he had the sense that he was losing her, that she was slipping back into her earlier preoccupation with the terrible events of the past month—her brutal degradation at the hands of men who were little more than animals.

He wanted to make her realize that her capture and treatment afterward was in the past. All that mattered now was what lay ahead of her. She knew for sure she was not pregnant, so there was no need to contend with that complication.

He was pouring himself another glass of rye and lifting it to his lips when a sudden thought crossed his mind. He peered at the glass of rye in his hand, grinned suddenly, then poured the contents of the glass back into the bottle. Stoppering it, he paid for it at the bar and took the bottle with him up to his room. Once inside it, he lit his lamp and stripped himself naked, pulling off his boots and peeling off his socks. Then he poured water from his room's pitcher into the china basin on the commode. Using liberal portions of the rye, he spiked the water. Dipping a washrag into the mixture, he

102

rubbed himself down thoroughly from hairline to crotch and well past his shins. The rye caused his skin to glow some, and as he worked, he gargled small doses of rye.

His whore's bath completed, he slipped into his pants and, with the bottle of whiskey in his hand, stole down the corridor to Roberta's room and rapped softly. He heard her stirring in her sheets.

"Who is it?" she asked softly, like a scared little girl.

"Who do you think it is?"

"Longarm?"

"Open up or I'll die of shame out here!"

He heard her approach the door, then unlock it. When she pulled it back, he saw that her hair was combed out clear to her narrow hips. And all she was wearing was one of the extra shirts Esteban had given her for the journey. The shirttails barely covered her flaring hips.

Shoving the bottle at her, he said, "Take a swallow. It'll freshen your breath."

Frowning, she took it from him as he stepped in and closed the door. "Longarm, what is the meaning of this?"

"You mean you don't know?"

"Oh, God, Longarm. I just don't know if I—"

"Take a swig."

She hesitated then lifted the bottle to her lips and took a small sip. She made a face and gave the bottle back.

"You remember what you told me in Caborca?" Longarm asked.

She frowned.

"You said you weren't ruined, and that if I gave you half a chance you'd prove it."

"Yes, I said that. I remember. I was so angry that you were going back without me—that you were going to leave me."

"I had no such intention, Roberta."

"Then why did you . . . ?"

She didn't need to ask the question. Even as she formed it, she knew the answer.

He grinned at her.

"You just did it to make me angry enough to go with you!" she said.

"And it worked."

"Let me have that bottle."

He handed it to her. "Go easy. That's the last bottle of Maryland rye they had down there."

"Never you mind. You've probably already had enough. Too much can ruin a man's performance." She tipped the bottle up, took another swallow, then began to cough. "Oh, my! That sends such a fire down into you!"

"It does that," he said, taking the bottle from her, then stepping closer and taking her in his arms.

She did not struggle, but the kiss she gave him was forced. He could feel her trembling in fear. He stepped back, then swept her up in his arms, strode over to the bed, and dropped her onto it. He peeled his pants off, then unbuttoned her long man's shirt and peeled it back to reveal her marvelous breasts.

"Oh, Longarm," she moaned. "I feel so confused."

"Do you want to?"

"Yes! But I'm afraid."

"That's understandable. Take another swig of the whiskey."

She reached over and took it from him. This time she

did not cough as she swallowed. Her eyes were blinking when she handed the bottle back to him. He took it and placed it down on the floor by the bed, then kissed her gently on the lips, very gently.

Gradually her lips softened under his gentle pressure. In a moment they opened the tiniest bit. He let his tongue run lightly just under her upper lip. She trembled, her arms snaking around his neck. He pressed his tongue in a little deeper and felt her hot breath as she suddenly opened her mouth wide and thrust her own tongue against his.

As if a dam had been broken, she thrust herself eagerly under him.

"You sure you're ready?" he asked, as he nudged her thighs apart with his knees.

"I think I have been ready since we left Caborca," she whispered fiercely. "I was just so damned ashamed of my need!"

"No more talk," he told her.

Enclosing her lips with his, he ran his hand down her back, then pressed her up into him. Roberta ran her hand down his side and worked it between their two bodies. Longarm felt her fingers on his growing erection. He twisted aside to give her hand more room to play. She squeezed him softly.

Longarm began to caress her breasts with his palm, feeling her nipples hardening. At the same time Roberta's hand was exploring Longarm's crotch. Pulling his hands away, Longarm bent to kiss her breasts' large brown rosettes. Their tips grew even larger under the inspiration of his hot, darting tongue.

"Now!" she cried.

He moved his hips carefully, entering her with gentle

firmness. Roberta gasped as he sank into her. He felt her body quivering. When he was in her fully, he lay quietly for several moments, letting her wet warmth surround him. Then he began stroking, slowly, easily, until he felt her relaxing completely, pulling him deeper and still deeper into her.

Still he moved slowly, never thrusting. The tempo of Roberta's breathing increased. The inner muscles of her thigh across his hips began to grow taut. Now Longarm increased the urgency of his thrusting. Roberta's body began thrusting up at him, responding to his faster strokes, jerking to meet him each time he went in.

"I'm ready," she cried. "Are you?"

"Take your pleasure. This is your night—not mine."

She was trembling on the verge of her orgasm. Longarm drove into her faster, deeper, each stroke longer than the one before it. Roberta's sighs turned to moans, then to a final throaty cry as her body convulsed under him, her hips jerking wildly for long moments before she sagged back onto the bed at last, exhaling a final gusty sigh.

He stayed in, enjoying the incredible warmth of her about his erection. She lifted her head and kissed him. Longarm opened his lips to her tongue and they melted together. He stroked her sides and lifted himself a bit so he could stroke her breasts. She began to breathe faster.

"I'm ready if you are," she whispered eagerly.

"All right then."

She planted a hand on Longarm's chest and pushed him back slightly, then moved to straddle his hips, her tight inner muscles holding him deliciously as she moved. In an instant she was astride him, straddling his hips.

"Do you mind?" she asked.

"I told you, this is your night. Whatever pleases you pleases me."

Longarm brought his hips up in rhythm with Roberta's rocking. He slid his hands down her sides, rubbing her soft skin, now moist with perspiration. The aroma of woman filled the hotel room by now, and Roberta's breast tasted pleasantly salty to Longarm's tongue.

Longarm let her set the tempo of her movements until he felt himself building. Still in control, he began thrusting up to meet her, and his response inspired her to move faster. She was soon past the stage of being satisfied with rocking. She crouched over him on her hands and knees, offering her breasts to his waiting lips, raising her hips high and dropping on him quickly, heavily.

Then she was in her final spasm, and Longarm let himself go, sank his fingers into her soft buttocks, and pulled her down onto him while he arched his back in his own shaking orgasm. Roberta fell happily forward onto him and lay quietly, murmuring in wonder and pleasure, the sweat from their exertions bathing both of them.

"You were just holding back to pleasure me, weren't you?" she told him, squeezing him affectionately.

"Like I said, this is your night."

"How was it, Longarm?"

"Wonderful. You see, you are a woman again. A lusty, healthy woman."

"It—it is so different with someone you like, someone who is a gentleman. All those beasts thought of was their own pleasure. I told myself I never would have sex again!"

He put his hand over her mouth.

"I want you to listen to me, Roberta, and listen good. Don't talk about what happened to you again. Not to any man or to any woman. Not even to yourself. It's over. Talking about it makes you think about it, and thinking about it is not healthy. What's past is past. All that matters is the future and those you love."

"Yes, Longarm," she said, resting her cheek on his massive chest and clinging to him happily. "I'll remember."

If there had been any doubt in Roberta's mind as to the warmth of her welcome, it vanished the moment her brother saw her approaching with Longarm. He flung down his shovel, and with Nathan following behind him, ran toward Roberta. She immediately lifted her horse to a canter and then flung herself from her horse and into James's arms. Suddenly shy, and wishing the brother and sister to have their reunion in private, Nathan drew up some distance back and waited. But soon enough Roberta beckoned Nathan closer, and by the time Longarm rode up, the three of them were walking happily back to the dig.

All that mattered to the two men was that she was back. A moment later, as they all gathered around James's tent, Roberta glanced at Longarm and smiled. Her cheeks were rosy, her eyes filled with joy. It had all been as he had promised her it would be, and she was very grateful.

Leaving the three, Longarm moved away from the tents and found Edward Pettigrew and Wynne doing their best to ignore Roberta's return. They were busy sifting dirt for artifacts. Using what looked like a screen door, they were shoveling dirt onto it, then shaking the screen back and forth, letting the sand and dirt filter down through it and leaving only the larger pieces to remain on top of the screen.

Longarm looked around them and saw a wealth of crockery, bones, and implements of various kinds. One large circular area had been pretty well excavated. It reminded him of something, but of what he could not quite recall.

Approaching Pettigrew, Longarm asked, "Where's Gladstone and his two men?"

Pettigrew drove the blade of his shovel into the sand and stepped back to wipe off his hands. He fixed cold eyes on Longarm. It was plain that by now he was completely opposed to the lawman. After all, he had struck his own son Wynne unconscious. Pettigrew was as dark as an Indian by now, and even Wynne's sun-scalded face had given away to a grudging tan. For his part, Wynne preferred simply to ignore Longarm's presence.

"Gladstone and his party have been gone for a week now," Pettigrew replied, his tone barely polite. "They are not archaeologists. Of that I am certain, and I don't care what that lieutenant told you."

"Then who are they?"

"I haven't the foggiest idea."

"Which direction did they take when they left?"

"It was in the middle of the night. I was not aware they had left until the next morning."

Longarm nodded. "Had any trouble with Indians?"

"Not since we returned from Lizard Gulch. But I can feel them about. I know they're out there. Watching."

Longarm nodded toward the butte looming over them. "You mean from the top of that butte?"

"I do."

Longarm nodded, satisfied. There were no Indians watching the excavation site. Pettigrew was seeing watchers, *miradors*.

"I assume you are all armed?"

"Of course."

"And your weapons are where you can lay your hands on them in a hurry."

"Of course, Marshal. But what are you expecting?"

"I'm expecting you to be able to hold off another attack if it comes. You might not be so lucky the next time."

"I am sure that with you here, Marshal, we will all be perfectly safe."

"I won't be here."

"Damn it, that's why you were sent out here."

"I'm going after Bird That Walks—and I have something to tell Tall Coyote's people."

"And what might that be?"

"How well their old chief died."

Pettigrew snorted. "Sentimental nonsense. I am sure he died as stupidly as do all these savages, in the act of killing some other poor, equally savage aborigine. Children, Marshal. That is all they are. Evil, disagreeable children who kill the way some children play with blocks. And Satan is their teacher. So much for your noble savages."

Longarm had heard all this before, from wiser and abler men. If he didn't happen to agree with it, he nevertheless refused to be drawn into the foolish argument.

"Just be sure you don't let Roberta get taken away from you again," he told Pettigrew quietly. "I'll have your hides if you do."

As he said this, Longarm glanced over at Wynne and

caught in his eyes a seething malevolence that made Longarm's skin crawl. But the look vanished the instant Wynne realized Longarm had glimpsed it.

The Pima brave who rode out to greet Longarm was not armed. Longarm pulled up on a slight rise to wait for him. As he glanced beyond the oncoming brave, he saw that the village looked well populated, with women, braves, and old men going about their tasks, and packs of dogs racing here and there. Farther down the stream a group of Pima women were standing in the stream's shallows, washing clothes. The sound of their laughter carried to Longarm on the faint breeze.

The village looked considerably more prosperous than it had when Tall Coyote left it with Longarm to seek out the renegade Bird That Walks. It was Longarm's guess that Bird That Walks had returned and was watching now from one of the lodges across the stream.

"I am Broken Feather," the brave said to Longarm as he halted his pony. "Why have you come to this poor village?"

"I left it with your chief, Tall Coyote. Now I have returned to tell his sons and daughters and fellow warriors how well he died."

The Pima moved restlessly on his pony. It would not be good manners—and certainly the spirits of Tall Coyote's ancestors would protest—if Longarm were not allowed into the village to relate the manner of Tall Coyote's death.

The fact that Broken Feather was hesitating was all the proof Longarm needed that Bird That Walks was in the village. Surely it was he who had sent Broken

Feather to send Longarm away. It was not fear, just good policy. Not until the memory of Tall Coyote had been wiped from the band's minds could Bird That Walks command any real following among these Pima. And Longarm was a fresh reminder of the old chief.

Nudging his horse forward, Longarm glanced back at Broken Feather. "Come," he said. "The hospitality of the People is famous. And I have a wonderful tale to tell. Your chief was great and he died as befits such a warrior!"

Broken Feather shrugged and followed Longarm across the river without a word. As soon as Longarm reached the village, the village crier approached on his pony, eager to learn the reason for Longarm's visit.

Longarm called out to him. "Tell the village I bring news of their old chief, Tall Coyote. Tell them to come and I will let them see in their mind's eye once again the bravest Pima of them all!"

His black eyes gleaming with excitement, the crier took out his drum and turned his horse to start through the village, his high, singsong call carrying far as he spread the news.

It was night. A great bonfire had been set blazing for the occasion. Longarm was to be the featured speaker. Bird That Walks had not yet appeared, but Longarm had no doubt that he was watching it all with great interest— and anger.

Broken Feather came toward Longarm and said, "The People wait for your words, Longarm. Speak now."

Longarm cleared his throat. "I was with Tall Coyote when he died. He was happy killing Apaches until one rose up from the ground and killed him with his lance. Before he died, Tall Coyote spoke of his people."

"What he say?" an old warrior in back asked loudly.

"He said he wanted me to get Bird That Walks for him and he wanted me to tell you how many Apaches he killed that night."

"It was many?"

Lying easily, Longarm held up the fingers of his right hand. A hush fell over the People.

"Why did he want you to get Bird That Walks?" another old warrior asked.

"He thought then the foolish braves who followed him would return to their home here by this great bluff."

Many heads nodded wisely. This sounded like Tall Coyote all right, thinking of his people to the very last.

Longarm cleared his throat and glanced quickly about, wondering when Bird That Walks would make his appearance. Probably many others were wondering the same thing. "I have more," Longarm told them. "Tall Coyote died without any mutilation. He lives now in the next world as one person. But now he looks down and sees what mischief Bird That Walks has caused, and he wants me to take him, as I promised him when he was dying."

"What you do when you capture Bird That Walks?" Broken Feather asked.

"I will take him to the white man's court."

Every Pima there shuddered. They knew what that meant, and they did not envy Bird That Walks. The Indian did not fear death. But the thought of imprisonment or death by hanging congealed his soul.

Broken Feather stepped forward. "We cannot deliver Bird That Walks to you. You must find him."

113

"He is here?"

Suddenly, in the distance, Longarm heard the faint beat of hooves, followed by the sound of splashing water, and then the fainter drum of hoofbeats. Bird That Walks was gone. Longarm was not the only one who heard the sound of the fleeing warrior. There was an almost audible sigh as the Pimas gathered around Longarm heard their troublesome chief flee the village.

"I guess he ain't here," drawled Longarm.

There was no response from the impassive firelit faces. Longarm turned and walked back to his horse, waiting for him beside Broken Feather's lodge. As he swung astride the animal, he glanced down and found Broken Feather standing beside him.

"Be careful, Longarm," said the new chief of the Pimas. "Bird That Walks is not like other Indians. Evil spirits have taken the senses from his brain. Now he has nothing to govern him but rage and fear. He sees what is not there and does not see what is there."

Great, thought Longarm. *I got a crazy Indian on my hands.* Longarm thanked Broken Feather and rode out.

Longarm picked up the trail of Bird That Walks early the next morning. It was heading straight into the mountains to the west. By that night Longarm was lifting into them, still on the Indian's trail. It was not lost on him that Bird That Walks was making no effort to cover his tracks.

Picketing his horse in a small clearing within sight of his campfire, Longarm fashioned a dummy sleeper with some rocks and his soogan, then took his Colt, found a tree that bordered the clearing, and climbed into it. He found some branches thick enough to hold his weight

114

and managed to wedge himself in securely enough to get some sleep.

He awoke a little before dawn to see a crouching figure circling the clearing. It was Bird That Walks, all right, only he was moving a lot more like a shadow than a bird. Tugging his Colt out of his belt, Longarm began to track the Pima. As soon as he did so, the shadowy figure disappeared, not to return again for the rest of that night.

But Longarm got no more sleep and was on his way early the next morning. He found no hoofmarks belonging to the pony Bird That Walks was riding and was about to give up until the Pima showed himself on a ridge a mile or so ahead, waited a decent interval for Longarm to spot him, then turned his horse and vanished.

The game continued for two days. On the third day, they were deep into the mountains. Longarm saw ahead of him a thin tracery of smoke lifting into the distant sky. It was mid-afternoon. The moment Longarm saw the smoke, he knew what it meant. Bird That Walks was beckoning him on. Longarm lifted his mount to a canter.

Chapter 6

Looking down from the knoll, Longarm saw a smolder-
ing cabin. All that remained standing was the fireplace
and the chimney. Beside the smoking ruin stood a large
horse barn, and beyond that, a long meadow with a few
horses and cattle grazing in the distance. Astride his
mount, Longarm made no effort to hide his presence.
After a moment, Bird That Walks appeared out of the
barn. He was dragging an old man after him. The old
man did not look like he was in very good shape. His
face was swollen and bloody. As the Pima flung him to
the ground, the old man appeared to cry out, but the
distance was too great for Longarm to hear him.

Then, in a gesture calculated to arouse Longarm's
fury, Bird That Walks kicked the old man in the head.

Spurring his mount off the knoll, Longarm charged
toward the small ranch, coming hard and straight on.

Bird That Walks ducked into the barn and took a position just inside the doorway, leaving the old man sprawled where he had fallen. Reaching the meadow at the foot of the knoll, Longarm pulled his Winchester from his saddle scabbard. From then on, he guided his horse with his knees. Charging across the meadow straight toward the side of the barn, Longarm checked the load of his Winchester, levered a fresh shell into the firing chamber—then abruptly changed the horse's direction and came at the barn from the rear.

He was less than fifty yards from it when a shot came from a ground-level window. Bird That Walks was not a good shot. The round whined past far above Longarm's head. Longarm did not wait for the Pima's aim to improve. He flung himself off his horse, slapped it on the rump to send it out of harm's way, then flung himself to the ground, keeping his rifle ahead of him in the grass. Resting his sights on the window from which the shot had come, Longarm squeezed two quick rounds into the sash, sending shards of glass flying.

But there were no more rifle flashes from that window. Longarm picked himself up and raced for the side of the barn. A shot came from an upper floor window and took a tuft of grass with it as it dug into the ground just ahead of Longarm. Longarm zigzagged to one side, then to the other, and kept going. He reached the side of the barn and flattened himself against it. A shot came from directly above, but it missed him by a foot or more. Longarm darted along the side of the barn until he came to its rear entrance and ducked inside.

There was a ladder in front of him. Dropping his rifle, he unholstered his Colt and clambered swiftly up it. From the rear of the loft came a rifle shot. The slug plowed into a pile of hay behind Longarm. Flinging himself to one side on the loft floor, he saw Bird That Walks rushing him, a gleaming knife held high. Longarm flung up his two feet, caught the onrushing Indian in the groin, then sent him flying over his head. The Pima struck the edge of the loft before plunging out of sight. Longarm raced over and was in time to fling a shot at the Indian as he ran out of the barn. He missed.

Dropping to the barn floor, Longarm saw the old man rise up off the ground directly in the Indian's path. A knife gleamed in his hand. Bird That Walks pulled up suddenly, startled, just in time for the old man to thrust his knife home. Gasping, Bird That Walks slashed just once at the old man, then turned and raced out of sight. Longarm raced out of the barn after him.

There was a side door leading back into the barn. The Pima ducked through it. That was a mistake. The slug he had sent at Longarm earlier had started a fire when it seared through the hay piled in the loft. The loft was fully ablaze by this time, and Bird That Walks was directly underneath it. Longarm followed in after him, crouching as he peered through the black smoke. A portion of the loft collapsed. A blazing ember caught the Indian on the shoulder. He threw it aside as Longarm flung up his Colt and fired. The Indian staggered but remained on his feet. Longarm dashed through the smoke. Emerging from it, he saw the bloody figure of Bird That Walks standing in front of him, bringing around a pitchfork. Longarm flung up his right arm to ward off the blow. The side of the tines caught his shoulder and flung him backward. He slipped on a pile of wet horse dung and went sprawling, his Colt clattering to the floor.

Partially dazed, he looked up and saw Bird That Walks looming over him. He still had the pitchfork and there was a grin on his face as he raised the fork over his head, preparing to plunge the tines through Longarm's throat. Longarm palmed his derringer and rolled over. As the tines slammed, quivering, into the floor, Longarm crabbed sideways and fired both barrels of the derringer up into the Indian's chest. Bird That Walks staggered back. Above him the burning loft finally collapsed, showering him with blazing hay and beams. In a second he was engulfed.

Longarm scrambled to his feet and fled the barn, the Indian's screams adding incentive to his flight.

The old man was still alive. Longarm knelt by him.

"Who the hell're you?" the old man asked.

"I'm a lawman. I was after that Indian."

"Did you get him?"

"It's more like we did."

"He was after you, that redskin. Wildest, meanest Pima Indian I ever did see."

The old man was bleeding from a deep wound in his side, the result of the one slashing blow Bird That Walks had dealt him. Longarm picked him up and carried him away from the blazing barn to a grove of birch and set him down. The old man was not going to die, Longarm promised himself, not if he had anything to do with it. Then he remembered leaving his rifle by the barn's side entrance and went back for it.

When he returned, the old man was dead.

Longarm was patting the mound of fresh earth over the old man's grave when he heard just behind him the crunch of gravel under a boot. He turned and found himself looking into the maw of a .45 caliber sixgun held by a young girl of twenty or so with long dark hair, a solid chin, and freckles. She was wearing Levi's, a ratty fur jacket, and a black, floppy-brim hat.

"Drop that shovel, you snake-eyed son of a bitch," she told him.

Longarm did as the girl suggested.

"Now step aside."

Again Longarm did as he was told.

"Ain't very talkative, are you?"

Longarm shrugged.

"Just tell me one thing before I kill you. Why'd you kill old Ned? He was a good-hearted old soul, never did anyone any harm."

"Didn't kill him."

"Then who did?"

"Bird That Walks—a Pima Indian."

"You lie, mister. Pima Indians don't kill white folks. Only Apaches do that."

Longarm shrugged.

The girl shifted her feet nervously as she peered up at Longarm. It was clear she was impressed because he didn't dance around protesting his innocence while he pleaded with her to let him live.

"Well," she said uncertainly, "if you didn't kill Ned, I suppose I won't kill you. But you got to admit, it don't make sense blaming a Pima Indian for all this."

"He was a renegade," Longarm told her. "His own people were glad to see him light out. He used Ned to draw me out, make me go for him. Ned did all right, though. He carved the Indian up pretty bad before I got a chance to finish him off. You all alone now?"

She nodded, her gun lowering, her face no longer

tough. Then her expression broke like a shattered windowpane and she was crying as if her heart would break. Longarm put his arm around her shoulder and let her cry herself out.

Once she got hold of herself, she told Longarm that Ned had taken her in three years ago, never laid a hand on her, and treated her like his own daughter. She had spent the last four days in the mountains west of this place looking for stray horses that had broken out of their corral a week ago. She had seen the plume of smoke and had ridden hard, only to find Longarm burying the old man.

"What's your name, miss?"

"Marylou. Marylou Breckenridge."

"Well, then, Marylou, let's get a move on."

"Where we goin'?"

"To see some crazy scientists."

Marylou didn't know for certain what Longarm meant, but she did not have any better plans—not right that minute, anyway. So, with a shrug, she turned and went back for her horse.

Longarm had not been seeing things. That had been Ma Titus and her son Clem he had seen crossing the tracks earlier. At the moment Ma and Clem were holding court in the saloon in Lizard Gulch's only hotel.

"They ain't no doubt about it," Ma insisted. "Pettigrew's got the map, and he'll have that treasure in no time, less'n you three no-accounts get the load out of your pants. I ain't shellin' out another red cent till you come up with something solid."

"Like what?" asked Smithers.

"You know damn well what! Gold! Maybe some of

them fancy crowns or headbands you were tellin' us about before."

Ma was addressing Percival Gladstone and Smithers. They had been introduced to Ma and Clem by Keith Masters. Neither Gladstone nor Smithers realized that it was Ma who had seen to it that Keith Masters had joined the fraudulent Yale expedition when it was passing through Denver.

The way Ma looked at it, there was no harm in killing two birds with one stone. Every cutthroat and highwayman holed up in the city knew that the Smithsonian's genuine expedition to the Sonora desert was after ancient buried treasure. Why else would Custis Long be riding shotgun, except to make sure nothing valuable got stolen?

Ma was determined she would see to that gold—and to that bastard Longarm at the same time. The trouble, at least from Ma's view of things, was that these two no-accounts from Yale didn't have the stomach for hard work. Which was no surprise, since they weren't scientists in the first place, and had managed never to work a day in their life if they could steal what they needed instead.

Gladstone shrugged unhappily at the bite in Ma's tone. "I swear, Mrs. Titus, all I heard in Yale was about the wealth of them old Indians, and them scientists who almost made the trip out here were pretty damn sure they'd be lugging back plenty of loot for the college. But I sure as hell ain't seen no treasure. Just pottery and old dishes and bones with rags on them. It makes a body sick, it does, to dig in such a place."

"You sayin' there ain't no treasure?" Keith Masters growled.

"All I'm sayin' is I ain't seen none yet."

"They was a mite excited the last time I rode out," Masters insisted. "They was excavating a large round building half buried in the sand. They called them pit houses, whatever in blazes that means."

"I say they're gettin' close," Clem said doggedly, speaking for the first time.

Ma turned to glare at her son disapprovingly. "If I want your two cents, Clem, I'll ask for it. Sit still and drink your beer!"

Clem, ducking his head like a whipped cur, shrunk into his massive shoulders and sipped his beer.

Ma looked back at the three men who were supposed to be representing the famed Yale University and fixed them with her small gimlet eyes. "All right. I'll take care of your provisions for another week. But at the end of that time, you better bring me something more than whinin' and complainin'. I know that feller from the Smithsonian has a map of some kind. Maybe you better just take it from him if you can't come up with anything solid."

"Steal the map?" Irving Smithers asked. He was so baked and strung-out-looking that everyone turned to stare at him, so startled were they by this sudden question. His words sounded as if they were coming through a dry reed.

"Why yes, damn it!" repeated Ma. "Steal the map!"

"Won't be no trick to that," offered Clem hopefully.

This time, for his impertinence, Ma almost struck him. Instead, she ignored her son and told Smithers, "Just be sure you do it before Longarm gets back."

"You still want us to tell you when he returns?"

"Yes. If that crazy Bird That Walks don't kill him,

we'll have to do it ourselves."

"How much whiskey did you give that fool Indian?"

"Enough to fry his brains, seems like." Ma finished her beer and stood up. "Good night, gents."

She turned then and strode from the saloon, her big lummox of a son following hastily. Watching them go, Percival Gladstone let out a huge sigh.

"She's a hard woman," said Gladstone.

"And a deadly one," said Keith Masters. "You better not cross her."

"No fear of that," Gladstone said wearily, picking up his beer. He decided he would need quite a few more before this night was out. The thought of the trek out to that heat-shriveling valley was enough to fill him with a desperate, dry despair.

There was precious little beer at that godforsaken dig.

As Longarm and Marylou entered the valley, Longarm noted that the members of the Yale expedition were back. Their excavation site was about fifty yards farther to the west than Longarm remembered it being earlier. But that didn't seem to matter much, since it provided a nice wide buffer between the two competing digs. The Yale group didn't appear to be too busy, as usual. The thin, emaciated one, Smithers, was the only one working. He was out in the middle of a trackless stretch of sand and mesquite, hurling his pick at the earth in a kind of mindless fury. Keith Masters, the gunslick the two Yale men had hired, was sitting on a wooden box in front of one of the tents, pulling on a hip flask, his hat pushed down over his eyes, pretending he did not see Longarm and Marylou. Gladstone, the expedition's leader, appeared in his tent's entrance and without waving or any other sign of recognition, watched Longarm and Marylou ride past.

When Longarm reached the Smithsonian digging site, Roberta, her brother James, and Nathan hurried over to greet them. Roberta kept her eyes on Marylou as the girl dismounted, then glanced questioningly up at Longarm.

"Take good care of her, Roberta," Longarm said. "This is Marylou Breckenridge, and she is now an orphan, thanks to Bird That Walks."

"Longarm! Do you mean . . . !"

"Yep. You can rest easy, Roberta, and so can Tall Coyote. I got the son of a bitch, but not before he fatally wounded the old-timer Marylou was living with."

"Well," Roberta said, grim relief showing on her face, "I'm glad you got him."

Roberta put her arm around Marylou's shoulder and led her off to her tent.

"Sounds like you had a time with that renegade Indian," Nathan said.

"Let's just say he won't be giving you any more bother. And neither will any other Pima."

"I'm glad to hear that. Because that other team is back, and they strike me more and more as trouble. Real trouble."

"You want to spell that out?"

"Last night I caught one of them trying to get into my father's tent. I chased after him to see who it was, but it was too dark and I lost him. It could have been any one of the three, however."

"What was he after?"

"Beats me, Longarm."

"Maybe a sharper pickaxe?"

Nathan grinned. "Maybe so. They sure could use some proper tools. Believe me when I say it, Longarm. This team of scientists is not making Yale proud."

James Prescott finished wiping his face and neck clean with a bandanna. "I can't understand that outfit. They have no screen, very few proper tools, and their tents are of the cheapest manufacture. Furthermore, there's no rhyme or reason to their digging pattern. We've given them a potentially valuable site, but they don't seem to know how to utilize it."

Wynne came up then. From his manner there appeared to be a general lowering in intensity of his dislike of Longarm. Joining in the discussion concerning the Yale archaeology expedition, he remarked, "And all they seem to be eating are beans and salt pork."

Longarm decided to change the subject. "How're you doing here? Find any more bones?"

"Plenty of bones and crockery," Nathan responded. "But nothing to give us a clue as to their antiquity. We know ancient artifacts pretty well, Longarm. That's our speciality. But we have found no sign of any. And these round dwellings we have uncovered are most puzzling. They resemble the pit houses of the Anasazi, who lived much farther east, I thought."

"Show me."

The two men took Longarm over to an excavation. Pettigrew was busy shoveling out what appeared to be a cellar or a basement. Longarm saw at once the circular nature of the dwelling and noted where tunnels had been uncovered. As Nathan and James watched with Longarm, Wynne joined his father in uncovering a round fire pit at the far end of the circular dwelling.

"The people who lived here used roof timbers to cover their dwellings," Nathan explained to Longarm. "This meant there must once have been considerably more trees in the area than there are now. The climatic shift is probably what drove these people away. And that means it must have been centuries ago."

"Could they have come here from Atlantis?"

James Prescott hooted softly. It was clear he was not at all impressed by Pettigrew's theory that this valley had once been inhabited by descendants of the lost people of Atlantis. Looking over the piles of bones and artifacts all around him, Longarm figured these were just Pueblo Indians who had drifted too far south, then gone north when the land dried up. Like farmers leaving farmed-out acreage in the East and traveling west for new lands to despoil.

It was close to sundown, and as the three men stood there watching Edward Pettigrew and Wynne digging industriously through the detritus of ages, slowly but surely uncovering the circle of adobe bricks that enclosed this ancient home's hearth, Keith Masters rode past them, showing some urgency.

He was heading in the direction of Lizard Gulch.

Chapter 7

Longarm was sitting with Roberta and James Prescott around the fire, enjoying a cheroot, while he listened to Marylou Breckenridge tell of her troubles and those of old Ned as they tried to raise horses in the mountains west of the Sonora Desert. She described Uncle Ned as a stubborn old cuss who never knew when he was licked, but the experience had been more than enough for Marylou. She had already decided that a horse ranch was not for her.

"There ain't nothin' heavier," she allowed, "than a pitchfork dripping with wet horse shit. Or nothin' more ornery on a cold, wet morning than a heated-up stallion with no gal horse to cheer him up."

"So what are your plans, Marylou?" Roberta asked, with a wink at Longarm.

"I'm goin' to find a place that still has a stage line

and drive a stage. Like Calamity Jane."

"I wouldn't pay no never mind to them tales about that crazy Jane Canary," Longarm advised her. "No one ever did get it straight about her. Jim Hickock stayed as far away from that crazy filly as he could get."

"How's that?" said Roberta in surprise. "I thought she and Wild Bill were lovers."

Longarm laughed. "Calamity Jane was a calamity, all right. She had a nasty habit of giving her gentlemen friends a dose of the clap. That's why she got thrown out of Madame Moustache's parlor house in Dodge."

Roberta blushed and Marylou Breckenridge was shocked. It was clear to Longarm that this was not the way Marylou had heard it, and what she wanted was the romance of Calamity Jane, not the truth.

Wynne came over to the fire, but not to join those sitting around it. He came to a halt beside Longarm.

Longarm glanced up. "What'll it be, Wynne?"

"My father would appreciate it if you would stop over to his tent before you retire."

"Sure thing," Longarm said, getting to his feet. He stretched, then threw away his cheroot butt, telling himself he was sure going to make an effort next week to quit the filthy habit.

Or maybe the week after.

Pettigrew was sitting at his camp table. A lantern hung just inside the tent's entrance flap, the light enough to enable the archaeologist to write out notes on the day's progress, something he apparently did every evening before retiring.

"Thank you for coming, Marshal," Pettigrew said, as Longarm eased himself into a canvas chair.

"No bother. If you've got trouble, that's why I'm here."

"I am afraid I have not been very cooperative, Marshal, and I am sorry for that. This trouble with the Pimas upset me, but you brought back Roberta, and she seems to be in fine shape. We all owe you a debt of gratitude for that. Even if she has broken her engagement with Wynne, I care about her and I'm pleased that she is now back with us, safe and sound."

"If that's why you asked me over, you needn't have bothered, Pettigrew. Like I said a moment before, that's my job."

"Well, it seems we have another job for you, then. Did Nathan tell you about our nocturnal visitor the night before?"

"He did."

"Nathan and I thought he had been chased off before he stole anything of value. We were wrong."

"What'd he take?"

"A case of very valuable maps of this region—and of this valley in particular. I need them, Marshal. And I want them back."

"Nathan said you didn't get a very good look at whoever it was. That right?"

"Yes. But it was not that thin fellow, and I don't think it was Gladstone. He wouldn't have the nerve to come for it."

"That leaves Keith Masters."

"Yes."

"And he's halfway to Lizard Gulch by now."

"I saw him riding out this evening, Marshal. It seemed to me he was in a hurry."

"That's the way it looked to me, too."

"I must have the maps back, Marshal."

"Why?"

"They give me the topographical details of this part

of the valley, using that butte behind us as a point of reference. Without them, I have no real indication of the direction I should go in future excavations. In addition, some of those maps are priceless, since they were the handiwork of the Spanish missionaries who lived in this valley at one time."

"I'll take a ride tonight."

"Where to?"

"Lizard Gulch, if I can't catch up to Masters before I reach there."

"Then you don't think those maps are in Gladstone's possession at this moment?"

"No, I don't."

"I agree. That hired gun of Gladstone's has them."

"And if those maps are as valuable and priceless as you say they are, he's probably on his way to a buyer."

"Marshal, he must not sell them."

"I'll do what I can, Pettigrew."

Ma was furious.

"I can't hardly read these maps," she cried, flinging them down onto the bed and turning on Masters. "There's nothin' here about any treasure. You must have got the wrong maps!"

"These were all I could find."

"Well, you don't suppose they'd be foolish enough to leave that particular map where anyone could find it, do you? These maps have to do with that valley, but there's nothing on them about the Spanish mission. Go back and get the right map!"

"But they're suspicious now. I was chased when I took these."

"They saw you?"

"It was dark. They couldn't see my face."

"Then you've alerted them. They won't have that map in any place where you can find it. Not now." She shrugged wearily. "Well, damn it, there's nothing here —and I can't see myself backing you fools any more. I have others who will be more direct. Tell Gladstone to haul ass out of there. He's no help to me now."

"You want me to hang around?"

"When Gladstone and Smithers pull out, find a spot where you can keep an eye on them."

"I know a place."

"All right. Get back there."

A moment later, while she stood at the window watching Masters ride out of town, she saw a familiar figure step out of the livery stable and look across the street at the hotel.

Custis Long.

Masters told her that he was back at the other dig, and she had been expecting him. He must have followed Masters. That made sense. These maps Masters had taken were no good to her, but they were probably valuable to the scientists. And here he was looking for them. Of course, he could have no idea she was in town.

But if Longarm caught sight of Clem, that would alert him.

Ma grabbed her hat and hurried from the room. She left the hotel by the back door and hurried along the alley and into the rear of the saloon where she expected to find her son killing time drinking beer and leering at the bar girls. She was not wrong. He was in a corner with one of the hussies, a redhead with a big nose and crooked teeth. She looked like she was ready to devour the damn fool.

As Ma approached the table, Clem looked up and a look of dumb despair came into his eyes. The girl knew Ma. She pulled back away from Clem, looking with sudden anxiety about her, as if she were looking for a hole into which she could vanish. It did Ma's heart good to see the fear and respect her presence inspired in these two lazy no-accounts.

"Finish up that beer, Clem. You got to get out of here. I got me a visitor."

"Visitor?"

"Longarm."

At once Clem was on his feet. "Where, Ma?"

"Across the street, last I seen. Let's go."

Ma turned and left the saloon with Clem at her heels, going out by the same door she came in.

She returned to the hotel, but did not go back to her room. Instead, she climbed to the third floor and knocked on a door at the far end of the hallway. A gruff, sleepy voice answered, asking who in the hell it was.

"It's Ma Titus," she said.

The door was opened by a burly, unkempt Mexican wearing only the bottom of his longjohns. That and a gunbelt. The Navy Colt sitting in it was well-oiled and looked to be in excellent condition, the only thing about the man which was.

Ma and Clem hurried into the room. The Mexican closed the door and turned to face Ma. "Where ees that map? I wait here too long now, Ma."

"Where are your men, Felipe?"

"They wait for me in the desert."

"I don't have the map. We'll just have to forget it."

"You know where is treasure?"

"No. But those men from Washington do."

134

Felipe's eyes lit shrewdly. "You want us to go ask them? Maybe if we make them dance a little, they be glad to show us that map."

"That's the idea, Felipe. Now get back to your men. I'll join you later."

"Where we meet?"

"There's a butte near the diggings. Wait near the top."

"How long we wait?"

"Just wait, Felipe. There's some business I got to clear up here first. It won't take long."

"Two, three days, I wait. No more."

"Now you listen here to me, Felipe. You'll answer to me if you move on that dig without me."

The big Mexican ran a meaty hand through his untidy, graying hair and licked his lips. "Sí, Ma. We wait. But there better be much silver. My men, they are anxious."

"I've come a long way, too," she snapped.

With a curt nod, Ma left the Mexican's room, then left the hotel by the rear door. As they walked through the alley to the saloon, she glanced slyly at Clem. "There ain't no doubt in your mind what you got to do, is there?"

"No, Ma, they ain't. But I wish you'd tell me what you got planned."

"I've already told you enough. Just remember to keep that Greener loaded and handy, like I told you."

"Sure, Ma."

But Clem wasn't really sure of anything—except that Ma was out to get Longarm. Clem still didn't know why Ma wanted him to spend all that time playing poker. Used to be she found him with cards in his hands, she'd whup him good and proper. And carrying around a sawed-off shotgun under his coat was a real nuisance.

But he wasn't going to ask Ma any more questions. Not now, he wasn't. He recognized that mean look in her eyes. Whenever she was fixing to get someone, he was purely grateful it wasn't him.

When Longarm saw Keith Masters leave the hotel and ride out of town, he cursed himself for not being able to overtake the man before reaching Lizard Gulch. He contented himself with waiting a decent interval and then riding out after Masters. He overtook the man a few miles outside of town, spurred on around him, then turned back to meet him at the head of a canyon he would have to pass through.

As Masters came in sight, Longarm urged his horse forward until he was blocking the trail. Longarm chucked his hat back off his head and smiled.

Masters slowed his horse to a halt. "Howdy, Marshal."

"Howdy."

"Long way from the dig, ain't you?"

"You, too."

"Reckon so. Well, nice havin' this chat, Marshal. But I got to get back now."

"You mean you already delivered the maps?"

Masters's face went pale, but his eyes took on a hard glint. "I don't know what you're talkin' about, Marshal."

"Tell me who you sold them to—and why."

"You're full of beans, Marshal. I don't know what in the hell you're talking about."

"Get down off your horse."

"No one gave you license to tell me what to do."

Longarm dismounted, strode over to Masters, reached up, and grabbed the man's gunbelt. With one quick pull, he yanked the gunslick off his saddle, then stepped back to let him land with the greatest impact. Dazed, furious, Masters reached for his Colt. Smiling, Longarm kicked the Colt out of his hand, breaking a couple of the gunslick's fingers in the process. Masters howled in pain.

"Get up!" Longarm told him.

Masters scrambled to his feet. He looked mad enough to cry as he held his broken hand. "You'll regret this, Longarm."

"Who told you to call me that?"

"No one."

"Only my friends do. Don't do it again."

"All right, you son of a bitch. Or should I call you *Mister* son of a bitch."

"Who'd you give those maps to?" Longarm asked.

"You can pull all my teeth, you bastard, but I ain't tellin' you a thing."

Longarm checked both of Masters's saddlebags, then searched through his bedroll. Both times he drew a blank. So that meant Masters had found his buyer in the hotel at Lizard Gulch. But who was the buyer? Why would anyone go to these lengths to steal a few topographical maps of interest only to archaeologists eager to dig up bones and pottery in the middle of the Sonora desert?

It didn't make any sense.

Longarm looked at Masters. "I'm only going to ask you one more time, Masters. Who'd you sell those maps to?"

"Shove it up your ass."

"I could beat it out of you."

"Oh, please don't hit me! I'll just die if you lay a hand on me."

Longarm went over to where Masters's Colt was lying, picked it up, and tossed it at him. Masters caught the gun with his left hand. Longarm had not drawn his own Colt and Masters saw this at once. There was no question of Masters being able to use his gun hand, but he was foolish enough to think he could outshoot Longarm with his left hand. As long as the lawman had not yet drawn his own weapon, that is.

"Now, you'll eat shit, Longarm!" Masters cried.

Longarm ducked and crabbed to one side as he reached across his belt buckle for the .44 sitting in his cross-draw rig. Masters fired at him. The bullet went wild, ricocheting off a shelf of rock over Longarm's head. Longarm aimed and fired from his hip at the same time Masters sent another round at him. Masters's bullet slammed into the ground at Longarm's feet, but Longarm's shot went to its mark, the bullet shattering Masters's left wrist. With a howl, Masters dropped the Navy Colt and sank to the ground, both hands now close to useless, a low, steady moan coming from the big gunslick.

Longarm holstered his weapon and walked over to the man. "You're not only going to have trouble getting back up onto your horse, you'll have trouble staying on."

"You can't leave me like this! I'll die out here!"

"Yes, you will. I'll help you onto your horse and then tie you to him. How's that?"

"You bastard."

"Yes. But first I want to know who you sold those maps to."

138

"Shove it."

Longarm turned and strode back to his horse. Mounting up, he waved once to Masters and started to ride off.

"Wait!" Masters cried. "Damn your heart! Wait! I'll tell you!"

Longarm pulled his horse to a halt. Without dismounting, he said, "Well?"

"Ma Titus. I gave the map to Ma Titus."

Longarm should have been shocked, but he wasn't. So that *had* been Ma he had seen crossing the tracks. That she had followed him this far simply in order to bring him down did not surprise him. Ma Titus's venom was well known to all those who moved in her circle. But that Ma Titus should be in the business of buying stolen archaeology maps was something Longarm found more than a little difficult to understand.

"So Ma's around, is she?"

"And she'll make you dance, you bastard."

"Tell me and tell me straight: What in the hell does that old bat want with those maps you swiped from Pettigrew?"

"She didn't want those maps. It was another map she wanted."

"Another map?"

"One that showed the Old Spanish mission that used to be there."

"Spanish mission?"

"Yeah."

It was beginning to make sense now. A Spanish mission meant the Jesuit order. Longarm had read about them having to pull up stakes from this section of the country in a big hurry when the Spanish king got fed up with their machinations. From that time on, word spread everywhere that in their haste to haul up stakes, they

139

had buried the treasure their order was notorious for hoarding. More than one such mission had left behind fabulous stores of gold and silver plate, rather than take it back to Mexico City where the government could—and did—lay claim to one-fifth of it.

That map Ma wanted was the one showing the location of the Jesuit order's mission and its stores of buried treasure.

Longarm pulled his mount around and rode back to where Masters was standing by his horse, one hand a bloody mess, the other with its fingers bent painfully.

"Get closer to your horse," he told Masters.

When Masters had done so, Longarm leaned down with one hand, grabbed the back of Masters's shirt, and hauled him brutally up onto the saddle. As soon as Masters was forking the horse, his boots in the stirrups, Longarm bunched his reins and slapped the rump of Masters's horse as hard as he could.

The horse took off with Masters trying desperately to stay in the saddle. The man must have been in considerable pain as he grabbed at the reins with his two shattered hands, but he was too busy to cry out. Longarm was not pleased to be causing so much pain, but with a gent like Keith Masters, he didn't see where he had much of a choice in the matter.

Longarm saw no sign of Ma Titus as he rode through Lizard Gulch on his way to the telegraph office, where he sent off a telegram to Vail inquiring about the Yale expedition to the Sonora archaeological site. He wanted the names of the two professors and their credentials. He also wanted information on the senator from Connecticut, Bradish.

Then he rode back to the livery, left his horse there, and walked across to the hotel and registered. Handing the quill pen back to the desk clerk, he smiled.

"Which is Ma Titus's room?"

"Ma Titus?"

"Short little woman with mean, gimlet eyes. She's got a tall, not very bright son she likes to kick around. Her favorite color is gray."

"Oh, her. That's Mrs. Smith."

"Sounds about right. Which room is hers?"

"You a friend of hers?"

"It don't matter, sonny, if I am or not. Give me her room number."

"Twelve. Second floor in back."

Longarm thanked the desk clerk with a nod and lugged his gear up to his room. Then he moved down the corridor to room number twelve and knocked softly. It was Longarm's belief that the best approach was always the direct approach. He didn't like dark alleys. But there was no answer to his knock. He tried the door. It was locked. He leaned his head against the door and listened. Longarm prided himself on being able to hear through granite if the occasion demanded. But there seemed to be no one on the other side of this particular door. Ma was out somewhere—and up to no good, he was certain.

He returned to his room. It was close to dusk. He did not light the lamp on his dresser. Instead, he drew down the ratty shade and peered out around its edge at the street below. An extremely slovenly Mexican was riding out.

Longarm studied the man carefully. There was something troubling about this Mexican's appearance in the

141

same town where Ma was holed up. Ma had a rare faculty for putting the meanest of these careless killers at her disposal.

Longarm watched the Mexican ride out, noting that he was heading west in the direction of the Sonora desert. This could be important—and then again, it might have no meaning at all. Longarm remained at the window for close to fifteen minutes longer before he hit pay dirt.

Clem strolled up the street, as bold as brass, cleaning his teeth with a toothpick. Ma was not with him, but he knew that wherever Clem was, Ma would not be far behind.

Reaching the gambling hall across the street, Clem mounted the porch steps and found a rocker. Slumping into it, he rocked a while, still picking his teeth, then got up and went inside the gambling hall.

Longarm left his room and went down the hotel's back stairs, cut down the alley and across the street, entering the gambling casino through a door that led past a couple of rooms used for those parties who played for more than house stakes. Before anyone could tell him he didn't belong there, he was moving up the back flight of stairs to the cribs. Treading softly past the curtained rooms, he found a dark corner on the balcony and picked out Clem's figure.

The man had found a poker game lacking a fourth player and was now settled in for the night, it appeared. Longarm watched for close to an hour but caught no sign of Ma coming after her big, foolish son.

He was about to call it a night when a girl's husky voice whispered in his ear, "What're you doin' there, mister? You a peeping Tom?"

Longarm turned to face the woman. She was almost as tall as Longarm, with long dark hair combed out all the way to her waist. Her face was very weary.

"I'm looking in the wrong direction if I am," Longarm told her.

"I'm Tish," the woman said. "These are my girls up here. You can't blame me for wanting to protect them."

"Course not."

Tish stepped back to get a better look at Longarm. "You know, I've been retired for a while. But there are times when I get the urge to hone my skills once again. What did you say your name was?"

"I didn't. Custis Long, ma'am. Pleased to meet you."

"Madam would be more proper. And I am pleased to meet you, Custis."

Longarm turned away from her glance back down at Clem. He was still deep in the poker game, all four of the players nearly out of sight in the blue swirl of cigar smoke that hung above their table.

"What's so interesting down there?" Tish asked, leaning her long body close to his.

He glanced back at her. She was purring like a big cat, and he was beginning to get the message himself. "Nothing," he said, "when compared to what's up here."

"You devil," she said. "I really shouldn't mix business with pleasure, but you look much more appetizing than what usually finds its way through that saloon door."

Longarm placed a large hand over Tish's melon of a breast and smiled. "If there's nothing pressin' on your time, why not show me the way to your parlor?"

143

She took his hand almost coyly and led him down a short corridor and into her room. It was much more than a room—a small apartment, really—and the bedroom was an ode to sensuous excess. The walls were covered with red satin, the canopy over the bed was red satin, the rug was red also, and the bed's coverlet was red satin. And, yes, the two lamps on the dresser were covered with red lampshades.

"What is this?" Longarm asked. "An anteroom to hell?"

Tish chuckled. "Nice of you to notice."

She brought him a drink. It was red wine, naturally, and Longarm found it so difficult to get down, he sipped only a small portion and put the glass down on the nightstand behind the lamp. Slipping off his coat, he draped it over the bedstead, his rig out of sight under it, the grips of his .44 within easy grasp. With Ma Titus back in town, now was no time to take fool chances.

Next he took off his shirt, his boots, then his pants. When he finished peeling off his longjohns, he leaned back luxuriously, the silken sheets feeling good on his naked flesh. Behind her screen, Tish had been busy as well. Now she approached the bed without a stitch on, her pale figure bathed in a hellish glow. Longarm was beginning to feel inspired.

She slid under the covers and at once her skilled fingers on his dawning erection added naked anticipation to inspiration. Tish half-rose, cocked a long shapely leg over him, then leaned back, lowering herself onto his raging erection.

Leaning forward, she placed her palms on his heaving chest for balance. Then she started moving her pelvis astoundingly as he grinned up at her, admiring

144

the view. Her nipples were turgid and her breasts bobbed in rhythm with her rippling lower torso muscles as she moved in a way that an Arabian belly dancer would have envied.

She moaned suddenly. "I can't believe it! I'm going to *come!*"

As she fell weakly down against him, he closed his eyes and joined her.

Tish lifted off him and something in the taut feel of her body caused Longarm to keep his eyes closed. He could feel her watching him intently, and as he relaxed his body, he felt a strange, unnatural drowsiness falling over him. It was not disabling, but it caused him to remember that glass of wine, of which he had drunk so little. There was a slight metallic taste in his mouth.

Tish was still watching him. In that instant he realized that she must have assumed that he drank all of the wine—along with the dope she must have put in it. It would be best, he realized, if she continued to think that. Allowing his mouth to drop open, he relaxed enough so that the depth of his breathing increased. He felt Tish pushing herself all the way off the bed and stand for a moment, looking down at him.

"Longarm?" she called softly.

Longarm did not stir.

After a moment, Tish stepped back from the bed. Longarm felt it jounce slightly as she reached over to pull back the covers so that his sprawled naked figure would be completely visible. On light footsteps she started from the room. Peering out from under his lidded eyes, Longarm watched as she paused by the wall and pushed aside a portion of the drapes to reveal a hidden exit. She knocked lightly on the door. It opened and Ma Titus appeared, Clem right behind her.

Ma had her Colt, Clem a sawed-off Greener.

Longarm came awake fast. Reaching up, he grabbed his .44 and rolled off the bed.

"You tricked us!" snarled Ma, as she grabbed Tish to use the woman for a shield. "Let him have both barrels, Clem!"

Clem flung up the shotgun and emptied both barrels. Instantly the room was filled with feathers. Aiming carefully from under the bed, Longarm squeezed off a shot. Clem dropped the shotgun and slammed back against the wall. Screaming, Ma flung Tish from her and commenced firing at Longarm as rapidly as she could cock her weapon. Longarm was too busy ducking to return her fire, but Ma's cylinder was empty in no time, and Longarm rolled out from under the bed and flung a lamp at Ma. The kerosene splashed across the wall. The drapes went up with a sudden *whump*. Screaming, Ma dragged Clem out the door after her and slammed it shut.

Tish was on her feet by this time, beating frantically at the blazing drapes in an effort to save her room from the flames that threatened to engulf it. Longarm made no effort to help her. Pulling on his clothes, he armed himself and followed Ma out through the door. Scrambling down the back stairs, he burst out through an unmarked door into the alley.

It was empty. No dead or dying Clem. No Ma. Not even the sound of fading hoofbeats.

Then, from behind him, he heard someone groan. He started to turn. A gun crashed in the darkness. A bullet caught him behind his right ear, glanced off his thick skull, and crashed through a window. The force of it knocked him forward into the alley's muck, where he drifted off into a crazed, semi-conscious world. He became aware of men shouting and of blazing tongues of fire licking skyward just above him.

Ma must have had a horse waiting nearby. He heard, then saw her gallop past him, Clem flung face down over her pommel. Only dimly was he aware of her gray-fringed, wrinkled face peering down as she flung one more shot at him.

By this time men were crowding into the alley, shouting "Fire!" and yelling for a bucket brigade. Around Longarm a circle of faces materialized out of the blazing night, some peering closely at him, others standing well back. Longarm tried to get up, but he felt as weak as a kitten, and his head was still ringing like a Chinese gong.

Then Marylou Breckenridge pushed her way through the faces and knelt beside him.

"Longarm!" she cried. "You all right?"

"Get me out of here."

"Where to?"

"My room. In the hotel."

Standing up and demanding that everyone get out of their way, Marylou helped Longarm to his feet. With astonishment and a great deal of respect for the peppery young lady, the crowd pushed back to let Marylou and Longarm through.

Chapter 8

As soon as Longarm reached his room, he sent Marylou down to the saloon for a bottle of Maryland rye and anything that could be used for bandages. She returned with the rye and a clean apron the barkeep had given her, along with a pair of scissors to cut it into strips for bandages. She told Longarm she had heard word that the town marshal and his deputy were looking for him. The fire in the casino across the street had completely demolished the frame building, but the bucket brigade had kept the blaze from spreading to any others.

Marylou cut out bandages from the apron, soaked them in rye, then wound the whiskey-saturated strips about his head. While she worked, he sipped on the whiskey and she told him what she was doing in Lizard Gulch.

There was uneasiness at the dig, she said, because

Nathan and Jim had noticed some Mexicans in the area. Some of them had even ridden out to the dig and demanded things like food or tobacco, which Pettigrew had refused to give them. They were not at all friendly, even though they hadn't caused any trouble as yet.

Longarm listened intently, trying to put this new factor in with all the other crazy items circling around this dig in the Sonora. He remembered that Mexican *bandito* riding out of town and wondered if that Mex could have just finished talking to Ma. It was a long shot, but maybe not such a long one, considering Ma Titus.

The scalp wound protested the rye whiskey for a while, then settled down to a mean but steady annoyance. Longarm thanked Marylou and was stoppering the whiskey bottle when a loud knock sounded on his door. He got off the bed and reached for his hat.

"Come in," he barked.

The door swung wide and two men entered. One man was old with long, sandy hair and a paunch. The other was young and eager and sported whiskers to hide his pimples. Both men wore dusty stars and gleaming sixguns.

"You'd be the town marshal and his deputy," Longarm drawled.

"You guessed right, mister. I'm Marshal Tom Wicker and this here's Dan Forster. Now just who might you be?"

Longarm flashed his badge at them and the edginess in their manner vanished.

"You mind tellin' us what this's all about, Marshal?"

"Ma Titus is an old acquaintance of mine. I was instrumental in her son's death. For some reason she's

150

held that against me ever since. In league with that madam across the street, she just tried to bushwhack me. I think I got a piece of her son, but Ma got away. I'd appreciate your help in taking after them."

The town marshal looked uncertainly at his deputy, then glanced back at Longarm. "We can't do that, Long. Our jurisdiction ends at the town line. Now we heard your side of this business, we reckon you can go any time."

"Right decent of you, Marshal," Longarm said, striding toward the door, Marylou on his heels. "By the way, what happened to Tish?"

"They ain't found her body yet."

"She never made it out?"

"Nope. Went to hell, she did, right from that devil's suite of hers."

As Longarm rode out of town a few minutes later, he was still thinking over the marshal's reply. Tish had her suite with its hidden entrances and exits, a perfect setup for a badger deal or any other bit of deviltry she might care to engineer. Longarm had called it an anteroom to hell, and as it turned out, he had not been far from wrong.

"What're you thinkin' of, Longarm?" Marylou asked, as she pulled her horse closer to his. "You had the biggest frown!"

"I was thinking of the wages of sin."

"Sinnin'? Is that hard to do, Longarm? I been lookin' fer a chance at that for the longest time. And I still ain't had any."

"Be patient. Sometimes when it comes, it's more than a body can stand."

"I can't wait."

* * *

They overtook Ma early the next morning. As they crested a ridge, one of Ma's bullets took out Marylou's horse, sending Marylou tumbling into a patch of prickly pair. Longarm flung himself unceremoniously off his horse and sent a beaded lizard scurrying. Peering over the ridge, he saw Ma in some rocks off the trail to his right.

He ducked his head back down and glanced over at Marylou. "You all right?"

"I am. But that crazy woman put a bullet in my horse."

"You better finish him off."

Marylou didn't have to be told twice. She shot the horse, then scooted over beside Longarm. "How we goin' to do this?"

"You ain't going to do anything. Stay here and keep down."

"You mean you're going after that madwoman alone?"

"One man's worth two women. You know that."

"Hell they are. Besides, that son of hers might not be dead."

"He's dead all right."

"How do you know?"

"Look at the top of that hogback, just behind the rocks where Ma's holed up."

Frowning, she peered in the direction Longarm was pointing. "Oh yeah. I see it."

What Marylou saw was the freshly constructed cross and the cairn of rocks behind it, obviously covering a fresh grave. Ma had stopped long enough to haul her son to the top of that hogback, bury him, and fashion the cross. From that hogback she must have seen Long-arm and Marylou approaching.

"I'll circle around behind the rocks. Take her from the rear. You stay here now."

Grudgingly, Marylou nodded.

Longarm trotted back down a gully. The sun was deadly. He left the gully and fled across a cracked, parched section of land populated by scorpions and Gila monsters. There were no sidewinders in sight. They were too smart to get caught out in this murderous sun. He came to a pile of rocks, circled behind them, and clambered swiftly up the far side until he was in sight of the hogback. He saw the cross all right, and the cairn marking what he presumed was Clem Titus's grave.

But he didn't see Ma.

Then he heard Marylou's scream. It came from the other side of the hogback. Her scream came again, only to be cut off by a gunshot. With no attempt to hide himself, Longarm sprang upright and ran. As he was cresting the hogback a moment later, he saw Ma riding off on his horse, leaving behind the sprawled body of Marylou.

The next day, on the gray gelding Ma had almost ridden into the ground, Longarm brought the wounded Mary-lou into Pettigrew's dig. Ma had shot Marylou in the leg. The bullet had passed through, but the wound was clean and in this dry, hot air, there seemed little chance it would fester.

Longarm carried her into Roberta's tent and let Roberta take care of her. Then he sought out Pettigrew and found him just outside his tent, looking over some recently dug up artifacts, as he called them. Old crockery was what Longarm called them.

"Was it you sent Marylou to get me?"

"I did nothing of the sort. I merely remarked on the insolence of these Mexicans and the possibility that there might be trouble with them later if we weren't careful. Marylou was on hand when I spoke, and first thing I knew she had mounted up and ridden off. I had no idea where she was going. There's no one going to tie a leash to that young lady, Marshal. She goes where she pleases."

Longarm accepted that explanation. Pettigrew was right about Marylou. She was already sitting on Roberta's cot while Roberta was trying to bandage her leg wound.

"Tell me straight out, Pettigrew. You got a treasure map?"

"A what?"

"You know what I mean. A map that shows where the pirates or whatever buried their box of treasure. Like Captain Blood. Or maybe some Jesuit missionaries."

"Longarm, you must be mad. What on earth are you talking about?"

"I guess you don't have a treasure map."

"I most certainly do not. Such nonsense! And unless you managed to get those topographical maps Keith Masters took, I now have no maps of this region at all."

Longarm studied the man. There was no doubt Pettigrew was telling him the truth. The man might be foolish, even a mite silly from reading all the books he must have read, but he was honest. If there were a Spanish mission in the vicinity of this dig, he knew nothing about it—and buried silver plate and precious stones were the farthest thing from his mind.

Longarm thanked Pettigrew for his time and left him to see how Marylou was getting on. She was lying down on Roberta's cot, her face white, cold sweat standing out on her forehead, her eyes closed. Roberta took Longarm's arm and guided him gently from the tent so as to be out of earshot.

"What happened to her?" Longarm asked softly. "The last thing I remember, she was sitting up while you worked on her, chatting a blue streak."

Roberta smiled. It was a cunning smile. "Yes. I tried to tell her to lie back and rest, but she insisted she was all right. So when I finished cleaning out the wound and bandaging it, I let her do whatever she wanted. After three steps, she was woozy—after four, she was very, very sick. I think she'll stay quiet for a while now."

Nathan came over. It seemed to Longarm it was as much to stand next to Roberta as it was to see Longarm, though he spoke to Longarm first.

"Glad to see you back, Longarm. You hear about those Mexicans been bothering us?"

"I heard. That's why Marylou came after me."

Roberta laughed softly. "Now, Longarm," she said banteringly, "you know that to inform you of a band of pesky Mexicans isn't the only reason Marylou rode clear to Lizard Gulch."

"Never mind that," Longarm told her. "Where can I find those Mexicans? Are they camped near here?"

James Prescott and Wynne had walked over by this time. Jim heard the question and spoke up quickly. "I did some reconnoitering this morning and saw smoke from campfires coming from a dry wash about three miles this side of the butte."

"I think maybe I'll go take a look-see."

155

"Wait a minute," said Nathan. "I'll saddle up and go with you."

"No need. Stay here and keep your powder dry. I got a hunch them Mexicans think you are all digging for buried treasure left here when the Jesuit missionaries pulled out. To them fellers—and anyone in league with them—you are the workers providing the honey. So look sharp."

"Is that why Gladstone and Smithers pulled out?"

"I don't know, but I'll find out soon enough. Remember what I said, now. Look sharp."

James Prescott owned a pair of very sharp eyes, Longarm mused, as he looked down at the remains of the overnight campfire in the dry wash. But whoever had lit that campfire was long gone. He dismounted and inspected the dry, gravelly terrain and saw evidence of many horses, rocks splattered with tobacco juice, and many more signs that a sizeable party of riders had made this their camp for the night.

Hell of a place to sleep, though, Longarm mused, in the middle of a dry wash. Any kind of storm in the mountains west of there could turn the wash into a raging torrent. More silly prospectors had been drowned on the Sonora than lost at sea rounding the Horn.

He mounted up and glanced idly up at the butte now completely dominating the skyline ahead of him. Suddenly, he came alert as he saw sunlight glinting on metal, once, twice. He pulled his horse around and rode off down the gully, giving no sign that he had seen anything.

When the banks of the wash were high enough to shield him from anyone on the butte, Longarm lifted his horse to a canter. Once he was on the far side of the butte, he headed for it at full gallop until he was lost in its immense shadow. Inside a stand of scrub pine, he found a pretty broad game trail and followed it all the way to the top.

He reached the top without incident, wondering if perhaps he had been seeing things. The place was as quiet as an abandoned cemetery. Dismounting, he tethered his horse near a cholla bush, being careful to keep his horse well away from it. Then he walked to the edge of the butte and looked out over the valley.

Damned if it wasn't a fine, even spectacular, view of the full sweep of the valley. After a moment he found himself looking more closely at the terrain. The sun's shadows outlined an entire series of ancient irrigation channels and low stone dams, following the natural contour lines of the big gentle slopes. Here and there he spotted more of the circular outlines of other dwellings similar to those Pettigrew was now so eagerly digging up.

But directly in the center of all this, precisely where the tents of the expedition were now sitting, he saw clearly the outlines of other, far more modern dwellings. A long, rectangular foundation, for instance, marking out a fair-sized meeting hall or meeting house. Surrounding it were other, smaller squares and rectangles. Longarm was looking down at the Jesuit mission Ma Titus and those other so-called scientists were looking for with such deadly zeal.

Hell, there was almost no need for a map. If anyone with gumption started digging under those tents, sooner or later they'd come up with the Jesuits' silver plate and gold—and any other treasure they might have left behind.

* * *

Longarm heard the click of iron on stone. He turned. Roberta and her brother were riding across the butte toward him. Longarm waited until they got closer before holstering the weapon he had automatically drawn at the sound of their approach.

"What're you two doing up here? Trouble back at the dig?"

"No," said Roberta.

"We saw you heading this way and thought we'd see what was going on," her brother told him.

"Figured maybe we could help," Roberta said.

"I wish you two had remained back at the dig."

"Now don't be angry," said Roberta. "We were just trying to help."

Longarm shrugged. "Now that you're up here, there's something I might as well show you."

Roberta and James dismounted and approached Longarm. Longarm pointed to the valley floor and the dim, ghostly outlines of the mission traced over its surface.

"Your camp," he told them, "is right on top of an old Jesuit mission, from the looks of it. There's quite a few who would like to know that. Ma Titus and a few of her wild friends, for example. Let's get on down there."

"What's the hurry, Longarm?"

Something in James Prescott's voice caused Longarm to turn.

James's sixgun was pointed at Longarm's belly and from the well-polished look of the gun and the grim set to his jaw, he was determined to use it. Roberta did not appear a bit surprised. For a moment Longarm could not believe her duplicity, but after one look into her eyes, he could. She was ashamed, perhaps, even unhappy to admit to him her betrayal. Nevertheless, she was just as coldly determined as her brother.

It seemed Ma Titus and her gang of cutthroats were not the only ones willing to commit any crime to get their hands on the Jesuits' buried treasure.

"You in this with Ma Titus?" Longarm asked.

"I don't know who the hell Ma Titus is," admitted James.

"Then you are in this alone."

"Yes. And there's one thing you should know, Longarm. Roberta's not my sister. She's my wife. We've been after this treasure for more than a year now. When we heard about this expedition, we managed to tag along."

Longarm looked at Roberta.

She blushed. "I'm sorry, Longarm," she said.

"It's too bad you've seen what we have known all this time, Longarm," James said. "We wouldn't want you to tell this to Pettigrew. It might spoil everything."

"You're forgetting the Mexicans—and that Ma Titus I just mentioned."

"No, we're not. Let the Mexicans attack the dig. Let this Ma Titus do the same. They'll find nothing but old pottery and dusty bones. None of that matters. Not to us, anyway."

"Which means you have the map."

"Yes."

Roberta said, "I took it from Pettigrew before Masters got away with the other maps. Pettigrew never knew the map's significance."

"So you two plan to sit up here, wait, then move in when the time is ripe and dig up the treasure."

"Yes," Prescott admitted, doing nothing to hide his pleasure at the prospect.

Ignoring Prescott's revolver, Longarm turned and started for the spot where he had tethered his horse.

"Where are you going?" Prescott demanded.

"For my horse."

"Stop right there," Prescott told him nervously. "I didn't give you leave to get your horse."

"I don't need your leave to do anything, Prescott. And stop waving that revolver at me. You know damn well you don't have the sand to use it."

"Damn it, I said stay put," Prescott insisted.

Killing a man in the heat of anger was one thing. But few men were capable of shooting down someone they knew in cold blood. Prescott was not made of this stuff. He was a soft Easterner who had probably never pulled a trigger in anger in his life. At least, that was Longarm's hopeful theory as he skirted the cholla bush and reached for his horse's reins.

He heard Prescott's running footsteps, and before he could mount up, Prescott grabbed him by the shoulder and spun him around. Longarm was delighted. He lashed out, his clenched fist catching Prescott on the point of his jaw, knocking him violently back against Roberta, who was just reaching them. With a startled cry, she went down under Prescott, both of them landing on the cholla bush, crushing it beneath them.

The bush was covered with the pads of a really nasty cactus which appeared to be no more than harmless fuzz-balls. But they contained tiny, porcupine-like quills no wider than a human hair. As Roberta and her husband struggled wildly to extricate themselves from the bush, they only managed to pull each other deeper into it.

Roberta cried out in sudden, painful yelps, while Prescott groaned angrily as he tried desperately to extricate himself from this needle-like briar patch. In a moment their frenzy was painful to witness. Desperately they tried to rid themselves of the countless tiny thorns that now covered their hands, the backs of their necks, and their arms. Yet with each movement the tiny, hair-like thorns worked their way still deeper into their flesh.

Longarm picked up Prescott's Colt and stuck it in his belt. Then he mounted up and drove Prescott's and Roberta's horses ahead of him down the game trail. The two would eventually extricate themselves from the cholla bush, he reckoned, but they would be in no condition to go very far for a long time.

At the base of the butte, Longarm dismounted and searched thoroughly the saddle bags on both horses. Then he slapped the two horses on their rumps and sent them off at a fast gallop. Remounting then, he set out for the Pima village. He needed help, and it would have to come from the Pimas.

It was late the next day when he entered the Pima village and approached the lodge of Broken Feather. As he pulled up in front of it and dismounted, Broken Feather stepped out to greet him, while a tide of Indians streamed through the village to see what Longarm wanted.

Both men dispensed with the usual routine about hearts soaring like eagles at sight of one's old friend. And there was no offer from Broken Feather to enter his lodge and smoke his medicine pipe. Instead, Longarm handed the chief a cheroot, lit one for himself, and shared the match with the chief. Puffing on the cheroot with great pleasure, Broken Feather waited for the business to begin.

"Bird That Walks is dead," Longarm told Broken Feather.

Broken Feather's anthracite eyes regarded Longarm

161

impassively. The fact that Longarm was standing before him seemed to have made that announcement unnecessary, and Longarm felt a mite foolish as it dawned on him that the death of a rival chieftain was not exactly a tragedy for Broken Feather or the band.

"Bird That Walks was crazy," Broken Feather said abruptly, as if to set Longarm's mind to rest. "He take whiskey and money from crazy woman. He died in fire. Now only his shade wanders through other world. He is punished."

The fact that Broken Feather knew how Bird That Walks had died surprised Longarm. But the mention of the crazy woman—and that could only have referred to Ma Titus—did not. If she was the one keeping this pot boiling, then everything made a little more sense.

"I need the help of my Pima friend, Broken Feather," Longarm said. "That crazy woman is maybe sending a pack of *banditos* after my friends."

"Your friends? The ones who dig?"

"Yes."

Broken Feather's eyes lit at the prospect of action. "The Pima will not fight the white man. Only the hated Apache or the Mexican *bandito* who is like Apache when he raid our people. How many braves you need?"

"As many as you can mount up."

"It will not take long. But first we must make medicine."

"How long will that take?"

"Tomorrow morning we will be ready."

Longarm knew enough not to mess with an Indian's magic. If it took that long for them to set up their medicine and fill their hearts with black thoughts for the hated *banditos,* then so be it. He wouldn't argue. But he was disappointed.

He turned back to his horse and mounted up. "Come as soon as you can, then."

Broken Feather nodded.

Longarm turned his horse and rode out past the screaming children and the barking dogs.

Chapter 9

Ma had been nodding by her fire when Miguel rode in.
She stirred, got up, and left her fire when she heard the
commotion. Keith Masters came over also. Both his
hands were wrapped in dirty bandages, but he was able
now to grip things with his right hand, despite the two
broken fingers. He had been practicing with his Colt the
day before.

Riding toward Felipe, Miguel flung the male gringo
off his horse, and then the female. They both landed
heavily, with thuds that caused even Ma Titus to wince.
The girl cried out, the man who was with her moaned
and pushed himself to his hands and knees. They were
both in terrible shape and, as Ma looked closer, she saw
why. They must have landed in a cholla bush or something. Tiny pinpricks covered their faces and necks and
arms and from some spots she could see the tiny,
threadlike needles protruding.

"Hey!" Miguel cried. "Look what I find just now. They coming down to visit us from the top."

"So you just helped them along," Ma remarked coldly to the *bandito*.

"I know them, Ma," said Masters. "They're from the dig. They're working for Pettigrew."

Ma's gray eyes lit craftily. She moved closer and squatted beside the woman, who sat up and brushed her hair out of her eyes. There were tears of rage and pain and frustration squeezing out of the corners of her eyes as she regarded Ma.

"You look pretty bad, young lady. What were you two doing up on top of the butte? There's no bones or crockery to dig up that high, is there?"

Sullenly, the girl shook her head.

Ma looked at the fellow with her. He glared back at her and said, "That damned greaser had no right to haul us up onto his horse, then dump us."

"Miguel has no love for gringos," Ma explained. "Just as you have none for greasers, as you call them."

She got to her feet then and walked over to Masters. "Get them some warm coffee. Maybe these two can save us some trouble."

She went back to her fire, leaving Masters to carry out her suggestion. She liked Masters. He wasn't as stupid as her son, and he took direction well. His dutiful company these past days had eased somewhat the terrible heartache caused by the death of her son, a heartache that had stopped her cold. Only now was she beginning to revive somewhat.

Not long after, when her visitors had had a chance to clean themselves up some and rid themselves of most of the cholla needles, Ma told Masters to bring them to her.

"My name is Ma Titus," she told them as they squatted warily near her. Masters sat cross-legged just behind them. The Mexicans, by this time, had lost interest in the two gringos.

"Longarm told us about you," Roberta said. "He told us you were after the treasure, too. Is that right?"

Ma smiled, pleased. "Yes."

"Then maybe we can work together—against Longarm."

Ma tried to hide her eagerness to hear more. "And how do you propose we do this?"

"We have the map, and we know for sure where the Jesuit mission was located."

Ma glanced quickly at Masters. She could hardly believe her luck. For so long she had been after this map, had financed those two fools who were supposed to get it for her—and now here it was, just dropping into her lap.

"And what do you want me to do?" Ma asked.

"With your men here to back you, we can simply ride up to the digs, tie Pettigrew and the others up, and dig for the silver. According to the map, it's directly under Nathan Pettigrew's tent."

"There might be bloodshed," Ma reminded them.

"Just don't hurt Longarm," Roberta said.

Ma glanced in surprise at her. "Oh?"

James explained, "He saved her life. Went all the way into Mexico for her."

"I see. Well, I'm sorry, miss, but that son of a bitch is responsible for the death of my two sons. If I get the chance I'll kill him."

The words were spoken with such icy finality that Roberta shuddered visibly.

But she made no further protest and Ma nodded

quickly. She understood. This fine young lady didn't want Longarm hurt—not unless there was no other way for her to get her hands on the treasure buried on that site.

"Do you have the map on your person now?" Ma asked Jim.

"It's in my tent, under my cot," answered James.

Ma looked at Masters. "Tell Felipe we move out tomorrow. Sober the men up. And get the wagon ready."

It was close to dusk when Longarm reached the dig. Nathan and Marylou were the first to greet him as he dismounted.

"Roberta and her brother are missing," Nathan told Longarm anxiously.

"Their horses returned late this afternoon without them," Marylou said.

"They've been gone for three days now," Nathan said.

"I wouldn't worry about them," Longarm drawled. "They'll turn up. It ain't that far from the top of that butte over there. And when they do get here, they'll sure look a mess. But it will serve them right."

Pettigrew and Wynne had come over by then and had overheard Longarm's comment. Pettigrew seemed a mite put out by it. "Now, just what is that supposed to mean, Marshal?" he asked.

Longarm explained. It took a while, and when he had finished, there was only silence.

It was Nathan who broke it. "You mean, Roberta—and James—!"

". . . are married." Longarm repeated. "And they, like just about everybody else west of the Mississippi—

except you—seem to know all about this Jesuit mission and the fabled treasure buried under your tents."

Pettigrew snorted, "I heard the stories, Marshal. Of course I did. But I certainly never paid them any heed. It's all stuff and nonsense. There is nothing buried here."

"Can you be sure of that?"

"But it's absurd!"

"There have been cases of other Jesuit missions burying their assets rather than have the Mexican government confiscate them. The Jesuit order was, after all, one of the richest in the world at one time."

"You learn that from your reading too, did you, Longarm?" Nathan asked, a wry smile on his face.

"Like I said once before, it's my secret vice."

"It don't matter if there's any treasure here or not, Father," Wynne told Edward Pettigrew anxiously. "Roberta and James thought there was, and I gather we've got other visitors to worry about as well. Isn't that right, Longarm?"

Longarm agreed and told them what he had learned from Keith Masters. And then, to the best of his ability, he explained Ma Titus to them.

"Wynne is right," Longarm concluded. "Since every con artist, nut, and *bandito* in the state of Arizona seems to think there's great treasure resting under us, it doesn't much matter if there is or not. What matters is we're in the middle of a target area, and those Mexicans you've been glimpsing of late are going to make their move soon."

"My God, Longarm, what can we do?" Pettigrew asked.

"I've already done what I can. Sometime tomorrow

we will be joined by that Pima band. This time they will be acting as our guards. Meanwhile, perhaps we can start looking for the map Roberta took."

"Do you know where it is?"

"I have a pretty good idea. It wasn't in the saddle-bags on either of their horses. They've stashed it in the camp here somewhere—in one of their tents, more than likely."

"I dislike having to search their personal belongings, Marshal."

"Let me and Nathan do it, then."

"I'll help!" said Marylou.

It was Marylou who pulled the map from the box under Prescott's cot. They spread it out on the table in front of Pettigrew's tent. Though the map was concerned primarily with the location of Hohokum digging sites, in the lower right-hand corner of the map was a faint but unmistakable series of outlines showing the location of an abandoned mission town. And in one small corner of what appeared to be the outline of the mission church, there was a tiny cross—in the center of what appeared to be a small chamber, only dimly outlined on the map and barely visible. Were they not all looking for it, they would never have found it.

"It's there, all right," said Marylou, her eyes wide. "Buried treasure!"

"We don't know that for sure," Wynne told her.

"And we won't know," said Nathan, "until we track that room down and find out for ourselves."

"But when?"

Longarm spoke up then. "We don't have all that much time," he reminded them. Glancing at Pettigrew, he asked, "Would the Smithsonian be interested in such a find?"

"Of course it would."

"Then I suggest we start digging as soon as we locate the spot."

Even though it was dark by this time, Pettigrew had little trouble figuring out where to begin the dig. It was, after all, something he had been doing for many years. He worked swiftly, laying down strings tied to posts, triangulating constantly, his two sons figuring rapidly for him all the while. Less than three hours after they began, they started digging. All five took turns and an hour later, they came to a solid floor.

Carefully clearing the sand and dirt away with a wire brush, they came at last to a trapdoor. After more careful brushing, they uncovered a hasp. There was no padlock on it. They lifted the hasp and pulled on it in an effort to raise the trapdoor, but it wouldn't budge. Next they dug out and cleaned away all the dirt and mud jammed into the cracks around the edge of the door and tried again. It budged a little. Longarm tied a rein to the hasp and looped the other end around his horse's saddlehorn. Mounting up, he urged the horse away from the uncovered cellar. The horse dug in and strained forward. For a moment they thought the hasp was going to give way. Then the door creaked open high enough for the others to get their hands under it and pull it all the way up.

Lanterns held high, Pettigrew in the lead, they clambered down a dusty ladder to the room below. Marylou, limping painfully, was the last. The chamber was as dry as a tomb. Not a single drop of moisture appeared to have found its way into it. Pettigrew held his lantern up so they could see the walls.

There was a collective gasp. Cut out of the solid rock walls were long niches. Fitted into each one was a cylindrical box of a size and design that left no doubt as to their purpose. These were the caskets of the priests and other servants of the Lord who had died at the mission.

"Over here!" cried Marylou.

Pettigrew swung the lantern in her direction. She was standing by a great sea chest. They hurried over to it. This chest was securely padlocked. Ancient though it was, the padlock was solid. Longarm drew his Colt and shattered it with a single shot. Lifting the lid, Pettigrew peered in—then stepped back, an ironic smile on his face.

They all looked into the chest then. What they saw were robes and cassocks, and one huge cross, long enough to span the entire length of the chest. It was hewn of rough wood and contained no precious stones. Marylou's quick hands explored the brocaded robes and the rest of the chest and found no gold, no silver plate, no precious stones.

So much for the fabulous treasure of the Jesuit mission.

Yet Pettigrew was ablaze with enthusiasm and could hardly contain himself. To an antiquarian, Longarm realized, this was a find richer than he could have hoped for—never mind that it contained no wealth to make him personally rich.

"We must seal this back up," Pettigrew told them excitedly, "until I can return with enough people to catalogue everything that's in here and perhaps construct a replica for the museum. This is a tremendous find. In this dry atmosphere, there's a good chance these corpses will be almost perfectly preserved. But hurry. We have already let too much moisture in already, especially this late at night."

No one protested. Everyone there, including Longarm, respected Pettigrew's judgment. They climbed quickly out and a few minutes later, the trapdoor was once more shut firmly upon the burial chamber.

Then it was Longarm's turn to give orders.

"If anyone comes looking for treasure, we can show them what's in that sea chest. And what's *not* in it. So we're not in any danger if cool heads prevail. But we better play it safe. I'll take the first watch, Nathan the second, Wynne the third."

"What about me?" demanded Marylou.

Longarm looked at her. Marylou was still suffering from the effects of her leg wound and was forced to use a cane, but she shuffled about with astonishing speed and skill, her energy as boundless as her impertinence.

"You can take all the watches if you want," he told her.

"I just might do that," she announced and hobbled off.

"She might, too," laughed Wynne admiringly, as he watched her move off.

Longarm climbed to a spot on the ridge high enough to give him a clear view of the moonlit valley floor. As he slumped back against a boulder still warm from the day's blistering sun, his rifle leaning against his shoulder, he hoped only that Broken Feather and his band would get there in time. His brave speech to the others was just whistling past the graveyard.

Ma Titus and her *banditos* would attack first and ask questions later.

Their only hope was Broken Feather and his Pima band.

Just before dawn Marylou and Wynne came running to the sleeping Longarm with news of approaching riders. As Longarm jumped up and grabbed his rifle, he could

173

see the dark, spreading shadow of horsemen sweeping toward them across the valley floor, coming from the direction of the butte.

"Start firing!" Longarm told the others. "It don't matter if you hit anyone. Just let them know we're armed and ready!"

At once the defenders opened fire in a steady volley. But the Mexicans kept coming, their bread-loaf sombreros making fine targets in the moonlight. Selecting one large target, Longarm tracked him carefully, squeezed off a shot, and saw the shadowy figure slip off his horse. At once those riders behind him veered off. In that moment the charge was broken. Splitting into two groups, the *banditos* swept around the camp.

In a moment, however, they had regrouped and were wheeling for another charge. This time, in accordance with Longarm's earlier instructions, the defenders ran over and made their next stand lying flat on the top of the burial chamber. It was a few moments past dawn and there was enough light for them to see the oncoming riders easily now, but this time they kept lower in their saddles as they charged. As they swept past this time, not one single Mexican was hit.

It was daylight by this time and Longarm could clearly see the lead riders. One was Ma Titus. Beside her, only one hand bandaged, rode Keith Masters. And riding behind Ma were Roberta and Prescott, their horses' reins in Ma's hands as she pulled them after her. Ma must have found them on the butte, Longarm realized, and kept them—and now, for some reason of her own, was punishing them in a terrible, calculating way.

Longarm heard her shout an order. The *banditos* wheeled and galloped far enough back to regroup.

When they came again at the defenders, this time, instead of charging full on, they broke at the last moment and began circling the encampment like Comanches, most of them firing their rifles from their mounts with greater accuracy than could most marksmen standing on solid ground.

Longarm was sprayed by exploding sand. All around him hot lead was pounding into the ground, each salvo getting uncomfortably closer. A cry came from Longarm's right and Wynne toppled over. A second later Nathan cried out. Even Marylou was no longer filled with bravado. Instead, she was keeping herself flat on the uncovered floor, no longer attempting to fire back as the slugs whined over her head. Surprisingly, Pettigrew seemed unafraid. He loaded his Springfield with calm deliberateness and with the same care returned fire, round after methodical round.

And then the Mexicans were among them, charging recklessly through the camp, overturning their tents, kicking aside their cooking utensils. Out of ammunition, Longarm used his rifle as a club and, with a wild swing of the long barrel, knocked the closest one out of his saddle. Another flung himself off his horse and slammed Longarm to the ground under him, his bowie held high. Longarm rolled over, caught the man's wrist, and twisted. The wrist snapped like a dry twig. The knife dropped from his hand. Longarm snatched up the knife and plunged it through the Mexican's gut.

Glancing up, he saw Ma bearing down on him, her Colt cocked and aimed. She had him now. His Colt was empty. He had nowhere to jump, no place to hide. Suddenly a heavy body—all elbows and knees—rammed into his side and drove him to the ground just as Ma fired. Longarm heard a scream. Whoever it was who had driven him to the ground groaned and then sagged heavily.

Longarm rolled out from under the person who had knocked him down and saw it was Roberta. She had somehow managed to jump off her horse in time to push Longarm out of the path of Ma's bullet—only to take it herself.

As Prescott leaped from his horse and rushed up to examine his wife's condition, Longarm turned once more to face Ma Titus. Undaunted, she still sat on her horse quietly, this time fitting her long rifle to her shoulder as she sighted on him a second time.

Before she could fire, the war cry of the Pima Indians sounded. Glancing over, Longarm saw what looked like the entire valley floor carpeted with hard-riding Indians, a great cloud of dust sifting skyward behind them. In the process of dismounting, the Mexicans looked back over their shoulders and cried out a warning to their brothers, then leaped back onto their horses. Cursing in frustration, Ma sent one quick rifle shot in Longarm's direction, wheeled her horse and raced off with Keith Masters and the rest of her men, the Pimas in joyous pursuit.

As Longarm watched, he saw Keith Masters overtaken and shot from his saddle by one of the Pimas. Somehow Ma Titus appeared to be outdistancing her pursuers. In a startlingly short time the desert was quiet, the war cries of the Pimas had faded, the dust already beginning to settle. Longarm holstered his .44 and walked over to see how badly Nathan and Wynne were hurt. Pettigrew and Marylou were tending to them. Pettigrew glanced up and assured Longarm that neither of his sons' wounds were life-threatening.

Satisfied, Longarm walked over to Roberta and Prescott. Roberta was in her husband's arms, obviously in great pain. Longarm saw at once where she had taken the bullet—high on the back of the left shoulder, and it looked as if the slug had passed clean through it. Roberta would live.

"You didn't have to do that, Roberta," Longarm said. "But I thank you."

"Now we're even, Longarm."

"It appears so."

He stood up then and looked down at the two. "I have some news for you."

They waited.

"Using that map you took, we found the sea chest. It contained a wooden cross and some cassocks. That's all."

"No silver plate, no—no treasure?" Prescott asked, incredulous.

"Nothing like that. The X on that map indicates a burial chamber, tombs for those faithful clergy who died on this side of the ocean. Nothing more."

Roberta just turned her head away, while her husband tried to comfort her. Longarm could imagine their despair. At the same time, he hoped that a time would come when they would look back with wry wonder at this foolish quest of theirs for buried treasure.

He left them and, with canteen in hand, strode out onto the desert to see to the wounded Mexicans, some of whose cries for water were already reaching him.

Chapter 10

Standing outside the telegraph office with Marylou, Longarm chuckled and read the telegram again.

WHO IN HELL IS SENATOR BRADISH STOP NO RECORD OF YALE EXPEDITION TO SONORA STOP WHAT IS GOING ON THERE STOP GET BACK HERE AS SOON AS YOU CAN STOP MEXICAN AUTHORITIES DEMANDING APOLOGY FOR INTERFERING IN REVOLUTION STOP GET BACK HERE AS SOON AS YOU CAN STOP VAIL

Longarm handed the telegram to Marylou. She read it quickly, then handed it back to Longarm, a grin on her face.

"I guess your boss wants you back soon."

"That he does. And it's time for you to get back to the dig with that wagonload of supplies."

"Maybe."

"What do you mean, maybe?"

"I mean it is going to be dark soon, and I think maybe it would be safer for me to stay in town for the night—especially with Ma Titus still around."

"And where do you plan to stay?"

"You got a room, ain't you?"

"I thought you and Wynne were hitting it off pretty well."

"We sure are—and he's a fine young man. I might even marry him if he plays his cards right."

"What's that supposed to mean?"

"It means he ain't quite yet a man. He's gettin' there, but before I settle down to teach him the facts of life, I'd like a lesson or two from someone who knows. A real man."

"You got one in mind?"

"What're you doin', Longarm? Fishing for a compliment?"

Longarm grinned. "Just wondered what you had in mind."

"How come you had to wonder?"

They started back to the hotel. He didn't try to answer her last shot. She was too fast a draw. But she interested him, sure enough, and he was not going to pass up an opportunity to teach this little vixen a thing or two—although he had a sneaking suspicion *she* would more than likely teach *him* a thing or two. And that was a pleasant enough thought.

He entered the hotel lobby, walked over to the desk clerk, and asked for his key. As he handed Longarm's key to him, the desk clerk smiled at him. "Did your mother find you?" he asked.

Just as casually, Longarm responded, "Not yet. Did she leave a message?"

"No, she didn't."

"Did you see which way she went?"

"No, I'm afraid I didn't."

"Did you tell her my room number?"

"Yes, I did." He turned then and looked into Longarm's mailbox. "And your other key is gone. The other clerk may have given it to her. She may have gone up to your room already. Is that all right, Mr. Long?"

"Of course."

Longarm headed for the stairs. Before he reached it, he turned to Marylou, who had heard the entire conversation and knew perfectly well what was afoot. "Stay down here, Marylou," he told her. "Ma sure must have changed her tactics, the way she conned that desk clerk. Maybe she's actually wearing a dress—but I got a sneaking suspicion I'll recognize her when I see her."

"Are you going up to your room now?"

"Yes."

"She'll be waiting for you. You'll be walking into a trap."

"It can't be a trap if I know she's there. Now stay down here until this is over."

Whenever Marylou visited Lizard Gulch, so as not to cause any comment she carried her Colt stuck in her belt, her coat flap covering it. Now, suddenly, she flipped aside her coat and drew her Colt. It bucked in her hand twice, sending two short blasts of fire from its muzzle.

In the dining room behind Longarm there was a

scream. Longarm turned. Ma Titus, wearing a lavender dress and a silly-looking hat, toppled forward through the dining-room doorway onto the lobby's threadbare carpet. As she struck the floor, she involuntarily detonated her big Colt twice, sending two thunderous rounds into the floor.

Then she rolled over and lay still, her old, shrunken face pale now in death, her gimlet eyes staring sightlessly up at the lobby's ceiling.

Longarm looked out of his window at the dark street below, watching the undertaker cart Ma Titus's body to the rear of his shop. Marylou was sitting on the edge of the bed behind him, still quite shaken up. She had acted so swiftly, awareness of what she had done came only after she saw Ma Titus sprawled on the lobby floor. She was more than a little upset.

Longarm understood, and under the circumstances, he was perfectly willing to forgo the lessons Marylou and he had been discussing earlier.

"Longarm?"

"Yes, Marylou?"

"I don't think what I did was wrong."

"Neither do I."

"Ma had an awful look on her face when she drew her gun. She looked like she was crazy."

"She was. Crazy with hate."

"I think maybe she's better off now—if there's a heaven, I mean."

"And there just might be."

"She would have killed you, Longarm. It was only a few yards."

"I'm very grateful for your marksmanship."

"Then come here and show me."

"Are you serious?"

"Will you please, please come over here and show me? I need your arms around me. I want to be comforted. Then I want you to be my man—at least for tonight."

By that time Longarm was sitting on the bed beside Marylou. He covered her mouth with his. She clung to him eagerly, her mouth opening under his gentle pressure. He was perfectly willing, even anxious, to comfort Marylou if that was what she really wanted.

It sure as hell was what he wanted.

Watch for

LONGARM ON DEATH MOUNTAIN

one hundredth novel in the bold
LONGARM series from Jove

coming in April!

Explore the exciting Old West with one of the men who made it wild!